BEFORE THE SAFARI

....

BY

MILTON J DAVIS

MVmedia, LLC
Fayetteville, Georgia

MVmedia, LLC
PO Box 1465
Fayetteville, GA 30215
www.mvmediaatl.com

Publisher's Note: This is a work of fiction. Names, characters, places, and incidents are a product of the author's imagination. Locales and public names are sometimes used for atmospheric purposes. Any resemblance to actual people, living or dead, or to businesses, companies, events, institutions, or locales is completely coincidental.

Book Layout ©2017 BookDesignTemplates.com

Ordering Information:
Quantity sales. Special discounts are available on quantity purchases by corporations, associations, and others. For details, contact the "Special Sales Department" at the address above.

Before The Safari/ Milton J. Davis. -- 1st ed.
ISBN 978-0-9992789-1-8

Contents

LOOKING BACK

An author is not supposed to have favorites among his/her own books. Each tome is like a child they say, creations which you love differently yet equally. But I must admit that Changa's Safari is my favorite. Yes, I said it. The three volumes have been a joy to write because they combine my three great loves; history, fantasy and action. The research required to add authenticity to each tale is just as rewarding as the writing, for I often discover details that lead to more adventures for Changa and his cohorts.

One of the things that caught me off guard when I discuss Changa is the interest in the back story of each character. To be honest I usually start my stories with a bare minimum of background on my characters with the exception of the main character. I usually learn more about them as I write, for situations arise where I must fill in more details about the character in order to tell the story well. Readers pay more attention to characters than I imagined. I get many requests to expand not only on major and minor characters but also on characters that exist only within one episode. Two examples are Kintu, the powerful demigod who assists Changa in *The Jade Obelisk*, and Tula, the feisty shape shifter and Panya's companion in *A Daughter Returns*.

I have often thought about the event that launched Changa's journey, the death of his father Mfumu at the hands of Usenge, and the adventures Changa experienced before becoming a savvy merchant in Mombasa. This is where the idea of this collection took root. This book is not only a collection of previous stories but also new adventures. These are stories of Changa and his friends before they joined his crew and a few surprises as well. I hope you enjoy reading them as much as I enjoyed writing them.

---Milton Davis

THE PROMISE

The drums rumbled through the city, each beat striking Changa in his chest like a club. The people crowding around him mourned in various ways; some clutched their heads and moaned while others covered their tear-stained faces. They all reacted to the scene taking place before them, the execution of their kabaka, Mfumu. Changa tried to look away but the woman holding him pulled his hands away from his face. Changa closed his eyes then winced as the woman slapped his cheek.

"Open your eyes, boy!" she said. "You must see this. You must remember this."

"I don't want to!" Changa cried.

The woman's grip eased for a moment upon hearing Changa's words.

"You must," she said, her lips close to his ear. "He's your baba."

Mfumu Diop knelt on the packed dirt, his bloody hands tied behind his back. Changa could barely recognize baba, his face swollen and bruised. A warrior gripped the rope tied around his neck, pulling the cord tight. Changa looked beyond baba to see mama and his sisters on their knees as well, their wailing cutting through the constant drumming to reach his ears. They were flanked by more masked warriors armed with short swords and spears. Changa's eyes then focused on the towering muscular man standing beside baba, the execution sword gripped in his hands. The man wore a mask similar to the warriors, except the mask seemed alive on his face, shifting with expression. His upper body was festooned with gris-gris, his lower body covered by a bark kilt that fell to his calves. He paced beside baba, looking down at him like a hunter admiring freshly fallen game. Changa's fear and sorrow slowly slipped from his mind, replaced by anger and hate.

The woman holding him spoke again, seeming to sense the change in his mood.

"Yes, Changa. Remember this. Usenge the sorcerer. Usenge the betrayer. Usenge the usurper. Usenge the murderer."

"Usenge the murderer," Changa whispered.

Usenge shook the execution sword over his head.

"The ancestors have chosen!" he said. "Only the strongest can rule, and I am the strongest!"

The sorcerer gripped the sword hilt with both hands. Changa's body went stiff as baba managed to turn his head. His eyes met Changa's, and then his lips moved. Changa heard baba's words in his head.

"Avenge me."

Usenge grunted as he brought down the sword. As the iron blade cut into baba's neck, Changa cried out.

"Murderer!"

Mfumu's body slumped headless into the ground. Usenge twisted toward the crowd where Changa and the woman hid.

"The boy!" Usenge said. "Find him!"

People surrounding Changa looked down at him, hopeful expressions on their faces. They pressed close to him as Usenge's men advanced. A large man with a scarred face knelt before him.

"You are the true kabaka now. You must live to take your baba's place."

He looked up to the woman.

"Get him out of here, Livanga. He has seen what he needs to see. We will do what we can."

"Thank you, Enyama." Livanga touched the man's chest. "We will meet again among the ancestors."

Armed men and women surged by Changa and Livanga. As Usenge's warriors pushed their way into the crowd, Livanga wrapped her arms around Changa then backed away until they reached the edge of the bush.

"Come child."

"No!" Changa said. "I must avenge baba! I must save mamma and my sisters!"

"Not this day, Changa."

Livanga dragged Changa into the bush as the crowd erupted into violence. Changa tried to break away from the woman but her grip was too strong. He went limp, hoping his weight would force her to stop. Instead she dragged him, his legs scraping against the dirt and shrubs. He finally gave in, clambering to his feet then running alone as well as he could.

They ran until darkness, or at least Livanga did. Changa's legs gave out hours before. Livanga picked him up then continued running. It was well into darkness before the woman stood still.

"We are here," she said.

The destination was a thicket of trees and bushes on the slope of a steep hill. Livanga placed the weary Changa down on a mat of straw then sat beside him. Changa watched her as she took a deep breath then lay on her back.

"Sleep," she commanded.

Changa didn't obey. He cried, the image of baba's beheaded body and his weeping mamma and sisters haunting him. When he finally sat up he looked upon Livanga. She was awake as well, sobbing as quiet as she could. Seeing his aunt mourn comforted him; it was good to know that he was not the only person saddened by baba's murder. He lay down again, this time succumbing to fatigue.

When he woke Livanga squatted beside him, pounding bananas and peanuts together in a small bowl. She looked up at him, her face solemn.

"We will stay here as long as we can," she said. "When we are ready we will go to the east. Your uncle will take you in and train you."

Before The Safari

Changa said nothing. He took the bowl offered to him then ate slowly. He was not hungry but he knew he needed to eat.

"Why did Usenge kill baba?" Changa asked.

"Usenge is the servant of the Ndoki," Livanga said. "Together they defy the will of the ancestors. They are strong now, but one day you will be stronger."

"Baba was the strongest man I knew yet Usenge killed him," Changa said.

Livanga placed her bowl down. "Your baba was a great warrior and kabaka. His only weakness was that he was too kind to those he considered friends. He overlooked the weakness of those he loved."

Changa stopped eating. "Baba loved Usenge?"

Livanga nodded. "They were once close friends, almost like brothers. But as the ancestors showed Mfumu favor Usenge's resentment grew. We all saw it and tried to warn your baba but he was blind to it. When the elders chose your baba to be kabaka Usenge's resentment became hate. He went into the bush and sought power from another source."

"If baba loved Usenge so much, why did I not know of him?"

"Usenge fled long before you were born," Livanga said. "We thought the bush had taken him. If only that had been true. The Ndoki found him first."

Changa shivered upon the mention of the Ndoki. As a child the stories of the wayward sorcerers wearing the skin

7

of gorillas frightened him the most; to learn they were real almost caused him to whimper.

Livanga placed a hand on his shoulder to comfort him. "Don't worry, Changa. Once we get to your uncle you will be safe. Usenge's power does not extend beyond Kongo."

She reached into a dark place in their hut then extracted a braided leather bag.

"This is for you," she said.

Changa took the bag then opened it. He smiled upon seeing the contents. Baba's throwing knives were inside.

"Your mamma gave them to me," Livanga said. "These knives were made by your great grandfather Caungula. He was a great kabaka and powerful blacksmith. They possess great power. If Mfumu had used them Usenge would be a bitter memory."

Changa took a knife from the bag, inspecting the blades.

"I will use them," he said. "I will kill Usenge with them. This I promise."

Livanga smiled. "You must learn how to use them first, young shumba. Finish your food. We'll begin your training today."

They finished their meal then stepped into the midmorning sun. The morning mist had lifted from the bush, leaving the foliage cool and damp. Livanga guided Changa to a small clearing. She looked about before finding a thick tree at the edge of the clearing. She tore a strip of cloth from a blanket then pinned the fabric to the tree with a small knife.

"You will hit the cloth with the knife," she said.

"I don't need to practice," Changa said. "I can throw a knife."

"The knives you throw are hunting knives," Livanga said. "These are warrior knives. It takes a different technique to handle them."

Changa hefted the knife. It was heavier than those he was used to but that just meant he would have to throw in harder. He pulled back then let the knife fly. It hit the ground. Changa looked at Livanga in shock and Livanga smile back.

"Like I said, it takes a different technique."

She retrieved the knife then returned to Changa. She threw the knife with a grunt; the blade stuck in the tree close to the cloth. She began walking to the tree, Changa following with his mouth agape.

"Every knife had its own balance," she said. "The only way you can discover it is to throw it. Once you discover its pitch, you can concentrate on throwing it with accuracy, then with power."

"How did you learn to throw, aunt?" Changa asked.

"I wasn't always your mamma's servant," Livanga said. "Now try again."

Changa tried again, and again, and again. Livanga made him throw the knives the remainder of the day, only stopping to eat and rest. He slept soundly that night, the horrible dream of baba's death brief yet still intense. When he woke the next day, his arms were sore.

"You will throw again today," Livanga said as they finish their meal.

Changa moaned. "My arm is sore!"

"Do you think Usenge will care if your arms hurt? He will kill you anyway."

The sorcerer's name sent a surge of anger and energy through his small frame. He put down his bowl then grabbed the knife bag. The knife fell as it did the day before.

"I'm no better than yesterday!" he said.

Livanga touched his shoulder.

"How do you eat an elephant?" she asked.

"One bite at a time," Changa answered.

"Your meal has just begun."

That night Changa stared into the sky at the stars. He tried to distract himself by seeking the constellations the teachers taught him, but he saw the faces of his mamma and sisters, Bunzi, Kifunji. They were all gone; baba was dead, mama and his sisters claimed as Usenge's wives. He pounded his fist against the ground, fighting the tears forcing their way out of his eyes then running down his cheeks. He sat up then wiped them away.

"It's good to cry," Livanga said.

She sat beside him then draped her arm around his shoulders.

"Try to rest. We must be on our way early tomorrow. Your uncle is waiting for you."

"Will we practice with the knives?" Changa asked.

"Of course we will."

Changa drew his legs up to his chest then rested his head on his knees.

"Good."

Changa and Livanga journeyed five more days before reaching the outskirts of his uncle's realm. They walked a narrow path bordered by heavy grass, the bush cleared by human hands. Changa carried a knife in each hand, his eyes darting left and right. Livanga walked before him, her sword in her hand.

"We are being watched," Changa said.

"I know," Livanga replied. "Your uncle is very cautious. He is wary of Usenge, as he should be. He wants to be sure we are who we appear do to be."

They reached the midway point on the trail when warriors emerged from the bush with wooden shields and iron tipped spears.

"Put down your knives," Livanga ordered.

Changa knelt then placed the knives in the grass by his feet. Livanga did the same with her sword. Livanga extended her arms away from her body; Changa repeated the gesture. The warriors rushed in, surrounding them with weapons poised for attack. A tall, lean warrior wearing a leopard headband stepped forward, followed by an elderly woman draped in a leather robe covered with gris-gris. The woman carried a short iron staff which she waved around Livanga, then Changa. She stepped away from them both beside the warrior.

"They are real," she said.

The warriors relaxed, lowering their weapons. The lead warrior's stern face transformed to recognition and relief. He extended his arms and Livanga walked into the embrace.

"Sister," he said. "It is so good to see you."

"I came as I promised, brother," Livanga said.

The warrior released Livanga then went to Changa. Changa stepped away; he did not know this man.

"It's okay, Changa," Livanga said.

The man squatted before Changa.

"I am your uncle, Ngonga. You are among my people now. You are safe."

Changa smiled. "Hello, uncle."

"He looks like Mfumu," Ngonga said to Livanga.

"He is strong like him, too," Livanga said.

"He'll have to be," Ngonga said.

Ngonga and the old woman took the lead. They continued down the trail, the bush encroaching until the branches brushed Changa's skin. Then suddenly it dispersed, replaced by an abandoned city.

"What place is this?" Changa asked.

Livanga hesitated before answering. "Nkombo. It used to be our city and my home."

Changa looked at the crumbling homes with sadness. Grasses sprouted in the once vibrant streets; a stand of trees ruled the central market place.

"Did Usenge drive you away?" he asked.

"In a way," Livanga said. "When the war turned his way, Ngonga decided the city was not safe. We consulted the ancestors and spirits and they agreed. So we relocated to a place more favorable."

"Usenge will never come here," Changa said. "It is too far away."

"Usenge will go wherever the blood of Mfumu still flows," Livanga said. "We are still closest to the spirits. As long as we survive the spirits will not choose him. Even the Ndoki cannot change that."

Changa shuddered. "So he will come for me."

"He will come for us all," Livanga said.

They camped in the city overnight then continued their journey at daylight. By noon the bush gave way to a land of open fields and steep hills. Livanga touched Changa's shoulder for attention then pointed to the tallest hill.

"That is our home now," she said. "Cilombo."

Changa smiled. "It is a good name."

Once they reached the base of the hill Ngonga raised his hand and the party halted.

"Livanga and Changa, moved to the center of the line," he commanded.

Once they were in place he came to them.

"It's very important that you remain in place. Step in the footsteps of the person before you. Do not waver. The road to the hillcrest is filled with traps, physical and spiritual. Do you understand?"

Changa nodded and Ngonga repeated his gesture. He returned to the lead then proceeded up the steep hill.

Changa walked up the hill; his eyes focused Livanga's footfalls. The climb took much longer due to the care required, but they eventually reached the summit. Changa looked up to see not a city but a fortress. A palisade of thick trunks capped with metal spikes surrounded the grass homes inside. Wooden towers rose above the palisades, extending the observation for miles on a clear day. Despite the martial design, Cilombo radiated the mood of a vibrant city. A host of children scurried to meet them as they entered, followed by others with relieved smiles on their faces. Changa received particular attention, with some of the children and adults reaching out to touch him. He moved closer to Livanga, who draped her arm around him.

"Don't be afraid," she said. "You are among family and friends."

Ngonga led them to the center of Cilombo. The elders sat under the meeting tree awaiting them, twelve men and women wrapped in wool blankets sitting on low stools. Ngonga walked closer to the elders; Changa was about to follow him but Livanga held him back. She eased to her knees then touched her forehead on the ground. Changa repeated the gesture.

Ngonga knelt before the elders. An elder woman stood, shuffling to Ngonga then touching the back of his head with her hand. Ngonga stood.

"Mama Kifunji, the son of Mfumu is among us," he said.

The woman studied the others until her eyes met Changa's.

"Come forward," she said.

Changa stood then went to stand beside Ngonga.

"Changa Diop, the spirits have safely delivered you to us. We are grateful for their blessings. A long road lays ahead for you; one that will call on you to be stronger than you may think you can be. But Ngonga is a blacksmith that forges strong men. He will instill in you the ways of a warrior, and we will teach you what the ancestors will share. Are you ready?"

"I don't know," Changa replied.

Mama Kifunji smiled. "That is a wise answer. We shall see."

Mama Kifunji looked to Ngonga.

"Take him to the others. Begin their training immediately. Usenge grows stronger every day."

"Yes, mama," Ngonga answered.

Changa knelt with Ngonga then the two of them returned to the group.

Changa looked up to Ngonga, his face worried.

"Who are these others?" he said.

"You will train with your age-group," Ngonga said. "We have selected 9 boys who have displayed the skills to fight with you. They will be your brothers in peace and war. You will live and train together until that day you are deemed ready, then you will march together against Usenge. They will be you closest friends, your commanders and your protectors."

"What if they don't like me?" Changa asked.

"That is a foolish question," Ngonga replied. "This is a matter of duty."

Ngonga led him through the city to the wall opposite the entrance. Another gate loomed before them; Ngonga opened the gate and they entered. A long house occupied the center of the area. There were posts of various widths and heights lined on either side of the compound. Nine boys emerged from the compound single file, led by a young man wearing a red tunic that hung from his left shoulder. The boys and their leader met them at the center of the compound.

"This is Caungula," Ngonga said. "He is your cousin and your group leader. He will teach you our ways and supervise your training when I am not here."

Caungula nodded to Changa and he nodded back.

"I assume you've had some training," the young man said.

"Baba taught me wrestling and some sword play. Livanga is teaching me how to throw knives."

Caungula smiled. "No one throws knives better than Livanga."

Caungula stepped aside. "These are your brothers. They have been waiting for you. They will follow you to war, but you must prove to them you are worth following. It's not enough that you are the son of a kabaka. If you wish their respect you must earn it."

Changa nodded. "I understand."

"You don't, but you will," Caungula said.

Caungula stepped aside and the boys approached Changa one at a time, giving their names.

"Hosi."

"Kasinda."

"Muhongo."

"Lusati."

"Katahali."

"Kadimba"

"Kambundu."

"Kalei."

"Epalanga."

"Go with your brothers," Caungula said. "There is food for you. You will rest the remainder of the day. Tomorrow your training begins."

Changa looked to Livanga with questioning eyes.

"Go ahead, Changa. I will be here tomorrow. I promise."

Changa smiled then followed the boys to the long house. The inside of the lodge was sparse. Each boy had his own bed and a weapon rack. Wooden spears and swords hung off the racks; to Changa's disappointment there were no throwing knives. A large iron pot sat over an open fire opposite the entrance, a stew simmering inside. The aroma made Changa's stomach grumble. He made his way to the pot then filled his bowl. When he sat cross-legged by the pot the other boys crowded around him.

"We are sorry for your loss," Lusati said.

Changa nodded as he ate. He did not want to talk about the past few days.

"Is Usenge the monster everyone says he is?" Kalei asked.

Changa lowered his bowl then closed his eyes. The image of his baba's beheading filled his mind.

"Yes," he said.

"Leave him alone," Kambundu said. "He's hungry and he's upset."

Kambundu moved closer to Changa. "I am your cousin. Ngonga is my father. It is tradition that I am your second but it is your choice. Hopefully as we train I will prove to you that I deserve the position."

Changa studied his cousin. He seemed older than the others, taller and broader at the shoulders. He carried the serious countenance of his father, his intense stare making the boy uncomfortable.

"I am not your superior," Changa finally said. "You have been chosen by the others so I will trust their judgment. They know you far better than I do."

Kambundu smiled an expression that seemed awkward for his face.

"Rest, cousin," he said. "My father can be a hard man."

Changa smiled back. "Like mine."

"They are brothers."

The boys laughed and the others smiled.

The following weeks were a blur. Ngonga trained them hard from sunrise to sunset. Changa was so exhausted at the end of the day he barely had time to think of his loss.

It was only during the night in his dreams where he remembered his family. He dreamed of his life before Usenge's uprising, recalling his baba's strong hands and stern lessons, mama's soothing voice and the taunts and teases of his sisters that annoyed him then but now he missed so much. Often, he woke in tears and his new brothers comforted him. As Ngonga promised they did their duty, but the struggles of training forged them into true friends.

Changa stood in the circle as his brothers clapped a fast rhythm. Kambundu stood before him holding two stones with a basket of more beside him. Ngonga stood beside his son, his arms folded before his broad chest.

"Are you ready, Changa?" Ngonga said.

"I am," Changa replied.

"I expect better than yesterday," Ngonga said.

"You shall receive it," Changa answered.

Changa twisted with the rhythm, the movements fluid and dancelike. He eyes focused on Kambundu's hands as he swayed them in time. Then he threw the stones as hard as he could. Changa spun right then ducked left, the stones spinning by. Kambundu threw more stones and Changa dodged them, keeping in time. He lost himself in the beat, his martial dance keeping him clear of the stone. Then the rhythm stopped and he stopped as well. Kambundu stood still, his arms akimbo and his basket empty.

"Excellent," Ngonga said. "You are ready for the bow."

Changa straightened, his eyes wide.

"Uncle, I don't think..."

Ngonga glared at Changa and he fell silent. Kambundu rushed to his side.

"Don't be nervous. Stay relaxed. The arrows will come faster but you can do it. Focus on baba's hands and nothing else. Never move back; only side to side."

Changa nodded as he tried to keep from shaking. Ngonga returned with the short bow, a quiver of arrows hanging from his hip.

"Move away, Kambundu," he said.

Changa's brother's clapped. He swayed from side to side, his eyes locked on Ngonga's hands. His uncle loaded the bow then pulled back on the bowstring.

The first arrow grazed his chest as he twisted to his right. No sooner had he turned to face his uncle did he let the second arrow fly. Changa twisted again, the arrow flying by, missing him completely. He was about to smile when he saw his uncle aim for his legs.

"Jump!" Kambundu shouted.

Changa jumped, pulling his legs up to his chest. The arrow whizzed under him, but Ngonga was not done. He quickly fired another arrow at Changa. Changa uncoiled his body then arched his back. The arrow sailed over him as he touched the ground with his hands then pulled his feet over to the ground as well. His brothers lost their rhythm as they clapped.

"Changa! Changa!"

Changa smiled at them then felt sharp pain in his thigh. He jerked his head down; an arrow protruded from his left leg. He gripped the shaft as he fell to the ground. His brothers rushed around him, Kambundu reaching him first.

"Don't touch it!" his cousin said. "There is a way to remove it so there won't be damage."

Ngonga appeared, looking down at Changa in disappointment.

"Distraction causes death," he said. "That arrow could have been in your chest instead of your leg."

He looked at Kambundu. "Tend to him."

"Hosi, Lusati. Help me," Kambundu ordered. Together they lifted Changa then carried him to his cot in the longhouse.

"Bring me the cleansing water and bandages," his cousin said. He looked at Changa in sympathy.

"This is going to hurt," he said.

He slowly turned the arrow and Changa clenched his teeth, holding back the scream threatening to escape his mouth. Kambundu pulled at the arrow twice before finally extracting it. Lusati handed him a gourd; Kambundu doused a cloth with the liquid inside then placed it on Changa's leg. Changa fought back a cry a second time.

Kambundu grabbed Changa's hand then placed it on the cloth.

"Hold this."

Changa held the cloth in place as Kambundu took the bandages from Hosi then wrapped them tightly around his leg. He stepped back to observe his work then smiled.

"You must stay off your feet for a day," he said. "That means no training."

Changa smiled despite his burning wound.

"That is a gift. Thank you Kambundu."

His cousin waved his hand. "When we are at war we must tend to each other. There may not be a healer with us. You'll learn as well."

"I may not live long enough to," Changa said. "I think your baba is trying to kill me."

Everyone laughed.

"He's trying to kill all of us," Kadimba said.

"It's true," Muhongo said.

"We must be ready when Usenge comes," Katahali said.

The mention of Usenge doused Changa's mood.

"Yes, we must," he said. "I must. When he comes he will come for me."

"Come," Kambundu said. "We must continue our training."

The boys followed their elder from the lodge. Changa massaged his leg then lay back on his cot. His thoughts drifted back to the terrible day, Usenge standing over his baba, the execution sword raised. Mamma and his sisters sat between the sorcerer's masked warriors, their cries harsh in his ears. Then Usenge turned, looking directly at Changa through his mask.

"I see you, son of Mfumu," he said. "I am coming for you!"

Changa sprang out of his bed then hobbled to the others. Ngonga glared at him.

"What are you doing?" he shouted. "Get back inside!"

"I saw him!" Changa said. "I saw Usenge!"

"What are you talking about?" Ngonga said.

"I saw him in my dream," Changa said. "He said he was coming for me."

Ngonga's face was solemn. "We know."

Changa reached Ngonga, grabbing his arm.

"No, he is coming for me now!"

The sky rumbled. Ngonga's head jerked upward as did the others. Though the thunder rattled the lodge there was no storm clouds overhead.

"This is too soon!" Ngonga said. "We are not ready!"

Ngonga looked at his son. "Kambundu, bring Livanga here immediately. The rest of you get your weapons now!"

Ngonga knelt before Changa.

"I am sorry, Changa. We didn't have enough time. You will have to leave. You will have to run."

"No!" Changa shouted. "I will stay here and fight."

"You are not ready," Ngonga said. "Livanga will take you away then finish your training."

Ngonga looked away from Changa. Changa turned to see what took his attention. A massive black cloud approached from the west, stealing the sunlight as it advanced toward the mountain stronghold.

"Get your weapons, Changa," Ngonga ordered. "Hurry!"

Changa hobbled to the lodge, ignoring the sharp pain in his thigh. He secured his sword about his waist, through his knife bag across his shoulders then grabbed his short spear. As he exited the lodge Kambundu and Livanga ran to him.

The malevolent cloud descended on Cilombo then released its terrible cargo. Misshaped creatures attacked the inhabitants, grotesque distorted animal loping after everyone. Ngonga rallied his warriors with his bravery, attacking the creatures with his sword and knives.

"Come with me," Livanga said.

Changa pulled away from her grip.

"No! I must fight!"

Livanga grabbed Changa's arm then dragged him away. She kicked open the back gate to the training compound the pulled him into the nearby bush. Changa struggled as Livanga dragged him down the steep slope into the valley below. His struggling ceased as the sky above them darkened. He looked up to see a black cloud pursuing them. The cloud passed them then settled before them then dissipated, revealing three gorilla-like creatures with oversized teeth and claws.

Livanga shoved him away.

"Run!" she said.

Changa fell to the ground as Livanga charged the creatures. Three throwing knives flew from her hands, each striking their mark. The screams of the creatures cut through the trees, hurting Changa's ears. The boy stood then took out his knives. He was not going to run.

Livanga danced between the three beasts, cutting and slicing them with her sword. They swung at her clumsily with more strength in their efforts than skill. One beast collapsed, barely missing Livanga in its death throes. Livanga ducked and twisted to avoid the attack of the others, their efforts more energetic after the death of their cohort. One of the beast looked past Livanga to Changa. It screamed then leaped over Livanga, landing before him. Changa twisted as the beast swung a massive clawed paw at his head. He back flipped away from another swing as he did when Ngonga shot the arrow at him, grimacing as he landed on his wounded leg. Then he let a throwing knife fly. The knife struck the beast in the side of the head, releasing a stream of black blood which doused Changa. The beast screamed as it fell, tugging at the knife in vain. It was dead before it struck the ground.

Changa grabbed another knife as he ran by the dead beast. He saw the other beast lying in the grass; to his horror he saw Livanga lying beside it. She breathed, but her right leg was mangled. Changa reached to lift her but she held out her hand.

"Listen to me, Changa," she said between gasps. "You must go. We will not win this day and Usenge must not claim you."

"No!" Changa said. "I killed the beast! I can help."

Tears welled in Livanga's eyes. "No, Changa. You are not ready. If you were today would be a victory for us."

Livanga gave Changa her sword and her provisions.

"Follow this trail," she said. "Do not stray from it. It will take you to a village where you will be welcomed. Do not tell anyone who you are, for Usenge's influence reaches far."

"But I will be alone!" Changa said.

"You won't be alone," Livanga said. "You have my sword. I will be with you. You have your baba's knives. He will be with you. Most of all, you are baKonga. The ancestors will be with you."

Changa hugged Livanga's neck tight, something he wasn't able to do with mama and his sisters.

"I will return, aunt," he said. "I will kill Usenge. I will."

Livanga squeezed him tight. "I know, Changa."

They released each other. Changa wiped the tears from his cheeks. He glanced back at Cilombo, Usenge's dark cloud hovering over it. He looked and Livanga who smiled at him despite her great pain. Then he looked at the trail ahead. He took a deep breath, and then ran as fast as he could.

He never looked back.

OYA'S DAUGHTER

The waning sun settled behind the cluttered horizon as two figures stole from the royal compound of Oyo. The duo scaled the bleached mud walls encasing the royal palace and descended into the thorn bushes. They knew the paths through the protective plants by heart, crossing the distance between the martial foliage and the dry moat as agile as antelopes. They halted, waiting for darkness to exert itself over the barren market before climbing from the ditch and sprinting for the narrow alleys of the lineage compounds. The rest of their journey was easy; if they were recognized no one would stop them for not only were they royal siblings, they were twins.

They left Oyo, heading for the Sacred Grove dividing the city from the farmlands. They found their favorite spot despite the darkness and set about gathering wood. In minutes a small fire blazed between them, illuminating their faces. Panya brushed back her braids and smiled at her brother, happy to see him after his long journey. Oyewole grinned back at his sister.

"I missed you, Wole," Panya whispered.

"I missed you, too," Oyewole replied. "I didn't think we would be gone so long."

Panya's face became serious. "Did you kill anyone?"

Oyewole looked away, darkness hiding his expression. "Yes."

Panya clapped her hands. "I wish I was there to see it! Wole is a warrior!"

Oyewole's face reappeared in the flame light. "It is not like the warriors say. A man does not always die with honor. Most of the times he dies with fear."

Panya frowned. "You sound weak, Wole."

"Talk to me when you've killed a man!" he barked.

They fell silent and Panya scolded herself for angering Wole. They stole away to enjoy each other's company as they did when they were younger and she had started an argument.

"What else did you do?" she asked.

"After the battle we went to Yubaland," her brother answered.

"What?" Surprise rang in Panya's voice. "There was another battle?"

"No. It was a council meeting. That's why I wanted to come to the grove. There is something I must tell you, something you should know."

Panya tensed. A voice warned what was about to be spoken but she wished it away. It was too soon.

"Baba and Ladipo of Yubaland have come to an agreement. They have decided to unite as allies in order to exert control over all of Yorubaland. Yubaland has more wealth than Oyo but we possess more warriors. Still, it was baba's obligation to offer an agreement."

Panya closed her eyes. "What did he offer?"

Oyewole drew his face away from the firelight. "You."

Panya stifled a cry. She waited to make sure her voice would not tremble when she answered. Oye was now a warrior; she would be a princess.

"So, I am to marry one of the oba's sons."

Oyewole's quiet after her question sent fear racing through her. The moan she fought to prevent seeped through her lips.

"I'm to marry the oba?"

Oyewole's face reappeared heavy with sympathy. "Yes."

Panya jumped to her feet and paced, shock and disgust fueling her slim legs. "He's an old man, as old as Baba! I can't marry him. I'm to marry Adeniji."

Oyewole looked away. "Not anymore."

Panya pounded her feet against the ground, raising a small dust cloud. "He can't do this to me. I won't let him!"

"Why are you being so stupid?" Oyewole snapped. "You knew this would happen one day. You are a princess and I am a prince. Neither of us chooses who we marry."

"You won't have to marry an old woman," Panya spat back. "You won't have to leave home to be a beast for elder wives."

Oyewole scowled. "I knew I shouldn't have told you. You'll go back and start an argument with Baba and he'll punish me."

"All you think about is you!" Panya swung at his head with her fist and Oyewole ducked.

"How can you say that? I told you Baba's intentions. Now you can prepare yourself."

Panya stood still. "Yes, I will prepare myself. I will tell momma. She will stop this madness."

She marched out of the grove and back to the city walls.

"Panya, wait!" Oyewole tried to stop her but she ignored his calls. She loved her brother like no other but he could not help her now. The only person who could stop her father from committing her to the Yuba was her mother.

The gatekeepers looked puzzled when she appeared but they opened the gate without a word. Panya strode across the courtyard and brushed past the grim guards before the door to her mother's home. Adenike slumbered in her large bed under a kente draped window, her head resting on a jeweled ivory headrest. Panya went to her, shaking her vigorously.

"Momma, momma, wake up!"

Adenike snorted and pushed her hand away. Panya shook her harder.

"Momma! Wake up!"

Momma sat up suddenly and shoved Panya away. Panya fell, her butt smacking the floor. Momma rubbed her eyes then look in her direction.

"Panya? What are you doing here so late? Why did you wake me?"

"You have to stop Baba from marrying me to the oba of Yubaland."

Momma's eyes cleared and a sympathetic smile came to her face.

"Oyewole told you."

Panya nodded.

Momma patted the bed beside her and Panya came and sat. She hugged momma's waist and leaned her head on her narrow shoulders.

"I told your baba this would happen. I told him to let me talk to you first."

"Tell him I won't do it," Panya said.

"I can't."

Panya gasped. Her mother had never refused her anything, ever. The fear that entered her mind with Oyewole resurfaced.

"Listen to me very carefully, Panya," her mother began. "We are a family of great privilege. The ancestors and our people chose us to lead them. We have done well and in return they have blessed us with abundance. But we have an obligation to do what is necessary so our people remain strong. That time came for me many years ago when I married your father. It was not my choice. It was my obligation. Now your time has come."

Panya stared at her mother. This was not happening. He mother was not asking her to go through with this.

"No," she blurted. "I will not do it."

Panya's mother's face became stern. "I have raised a selfish daughter. You choose your own convenience over the lives of your people? If this marriage does not take place there will be war between Oyo and Yubaland. Many will die because of your selfishness. Your brother may die because of it. Is this what you want?"

"You talk to her as if she has a choice," her father said. Oba Jumoke ducked as he entered into the room and folded his long arms across his chest. He had never been a big part of their lives with his constant travels between his wives' homes. Adenike was the only wife allowed to live in the main palace, but the privilege didn't give her any more time that the other wives. Panya never liked the way he looked at them; his eyes seemed to access their worth. She realized that was exactly what he was doing.

"A marriage agreement has been struck between our houses and it will not be broken," he said. "The wedding ceremony will take place at the beginning of the rainy season."

His eyes shifted to her mother. "You will use that time to make sure she is prepared."

Her mother looked away. "Of course."

"Panya, come to me."

Panya stood before her father. Though her face was complacent her hands shook with anger.

"Yes, baba?"

"It's time you come to terms with your place. What you do will mean much to our people. Oba Lapido asked for you specifically because of your special birth. He will value you highly, which means nothing you ask will be denied. You will be his First Wife; you will control his household. I could not think of a better union for my daughter."

I could, she thought.

"Now go and let your mother sleep. I suggest you do the same. The next few weeks will be very busy for you."

Panya trudged out of her mother's room and across the compound to her bedchamber. She lay down and propped her head on her headrest. So she was to marry Ladipo and no one thought wrong of it except her. It was her duty as her father's daughter, her obligation to her people. It was the price to pay for a life of privilege.

Panya sat up, spurred by a wave of desperation. A wall had been erected around her, a barrier of tradition and duty. She was trapped like cattle and expected to behave like them, never testing the obstacle separating them from freedom. Panya would not give up so easily. If no one in her world would help her, then maybe someone of another world would.

The next morning Panya said nothing about the previous day's turmoil. She went to her mother as always as was attentive to her studies. Later that day she snuck off with Oyewole and they practiced hand combat. Women were forbidden from learning the secret fight style of Oyo's warriors but no secrets existed between Panya and Oyewole. She was more aggressive than usual but Oyewole didn't seem to notice. After their practice she returned to the compound, bathed then went to the market. She purchased a bolt of purple fabric, sandalwood incense and three red garnets. She also bought chickweed and three copper bracelets. As she walked back to the compound a hand reached from the crowd and gripped her wrist. A short, older woman held her covered in an orange shawl held her. The woman's face was plain yet compelling.

"Back, beggar," her guard barked. "You block the princess's way."

"No," Panya said. "She is fine." Panya smiled at the woman but her expression was not returned. Panya was insulted by the woman's rudeness.

"What do you want?"

"I should be asking you," the woman replied. She nodded her head towards Panya's items.

"You plan to summon her tonight?" she asked.

Panya's eyes narrowed. "That's none of your business."

"Just because you are daughter of the oba does not put you higher than all," the woman snapped. "Calling on her is no small matter, especially if you are not one of her chosen. You should consult with a babalawo before making such decisions."

"You've said enough," Panya decided. "Release me."

"Be careful, daughter," the woman advised. "Do not put yourself in a situation where you have no control."

Panya mouth sagged. "It would be no different than now."

She snatched her hand away and her guard shoved the old woman into the crowd.

The crone's words remained with Panya into the compound and back to her room, flittering in her mind like night flies. She didn't know what she was doing. She was desperate. For her entire life her status as the oba's daughter and a twin had protected her from any adversity. She saw no need to call on the babalawo's advice or the orishas power. But with no one to turn to she had no choice. Panya had no altar so she set the candles on both sides of her bed. She placed the purple fabric about her shoulders then placed garnets, chickweed and bracelets before her on the bed. Panya lifted her trembling hands as nervous sweat emerged on her forehead. This was foolish. Why should an orisha come to her aid when she had never called on her before, especially one as powerful as Oya? The market woman's words returned, jumbling in her head like an acrobat.

She was about to douse the candles when a breeze swept through the room. The flames bounced about and flared in its presence.

"Oya?" Panya looked about her room as if searching for an intruder. The breeze swirled around her, lifting the colored fabric from her arms. Oya was present, she thought. She had to go through with it. Panya closed her eyes and lifted her hands high.

Oya, Lady of Storms,
Bringer of Change,
Warrior Woman,

Orisha that summons the winds and protects the dead,
Ruler of tempest and thunder,
Please hear me this night.
Help me, Oya
Help me.

The breeze swelled into wind. It swirled about her tightly, pinning her arms to her sides. Panya's heart hammered her chest and her eyes grew wide. She wanted to run but the spinning winds held her still. Nothing else moved in her room; the candles licked lazily at the darkness, the sheets on her bed lay still. The wind spun faster and she rose into the air. Then it eased, a cocoon of calm surrounding her. Inches from her face the air moved. She was in Oya's hands.

When she first tried to speak her voiced cracked in her dry throat. She swallowed before speaking again.

"Oya, I need your help. I am to be married to a man that I have not chosen. I am told that our union will bring peace to our people. I do not wish to marry him. I beg you to stop this marriage. If you do so, I will honor you with libations and praise. I will be your daughter."

Panya did not know what to expect. Would Oya speak to her? Would she plant a vision in her head? When the answer came it was as clear as it was vague. Warm air gently pressed against her skin, reminding her of her mother's hands. Panya smiled as she drifted down. When her feet touched the floor, the wind burst from her room, blowing out the flames and toppling the candles. Panya smiled and collapsed exhausted onto her bed. Oya had come. Oya would help her.

Panya's behavior over the passing weeks was typical of a young woman preparing for marriage. She became her mother's shadow, listening intensely as she shared the wisdom and duties of a royal wife. Panya spent long days with the seamstresses as they created her wedding dress and head wrap from the finest fabric in the kingdom. Her mood was at times solemn and at other times joyful. Though she had moments of dread they quickly passed. Oya had come to her. Oya would not allow the wedding to occur.

Panya stood on a low stool surrounded by a gaggle of seamstresses. They talked excitedly as they arranged bolts of fabric around her, each one trying to exert her design vision over the other. Panya smiled pleasantly at all of them. It didn't matter what they chose; it would all be in vain. Just as she was about to make a selection the door swung open and Oyewole entered. Panya recognized his expression immediately and the smile melted. The seamstresses prostrated before him, their strips of cloth dangling from Panya's shoulders.

"Leave us," he commanded.

The women scrambled to their feet and hurried from the room. Oyewole strode up to her, oblivious to her near nakedness. Panya clutched the fabric around her, anger growing as her brother confronted her.

"What are you up to, Panya?"

Panya stepped down from the stood and stood before her brother, their noses almost touching.

"What does it look like? I'm preparing for my wedding."

"Don't play with me. A few weeks ago, you were sick about this marriage now you float about as if it's a dream come true."

"Turn around!" Panya said. Oyewole's eyes widened then closed as he looked away.

"I'm sorry," he said.

Panya discarded the scraps of fabric and dressed. "How should I behave? I am to be married whether I agree or not. I might as well enjoy the process. It only happens once."

"You could run away," Oyewole suggested.

His words hit her like a whipping stick. "Run away? Run away?"

Panya searched her brother's face for any sign of sarcasm but found none. He was serious, which made her angry.

"You speak like I'm a child! Run away? Where would I go? What would I do when I got where ever I ran off to? How long would it take for Baba to find me?"

Oyewole didn't reply. His face seemed sad, no, remorseful. Panya's anger subsided. Worry wrinkled her brow despite her confidence in Oya's promise.

"What is wrong, Wole?"

Oyewole opened his mouth then suddenly closed it. He rushed up to her and held her tight. Panya felt a warm tear on her shoulder. She tried to pull away but Oyewole held her tight.

"Remember everything I taught you," he whispered.

He let her go and turned away before she could see his face. Panya watched him leave the room, confusion holding her in place. When she regained her movement Oyewole had disappeared.

* * *

The day had come. Oyo was dressed in full splendor, its towers freshly whitewashed, and golden banners waving with the early rainy season breeze. The royal courtyard teemed with elders, dignitaries and spectators, all present to witness the marriage of Panya and the union of two powerful kingdoms. Panya's mother and father sat side by side in their thrones, both draped in matching green robes and headdress. The wedding party could be heard approaching, their songs rising above the city walls and settling among the wedding party. They had been outside the walls for an hour, her father exercising his right to make them wait as long as he felt necessary. This was no normal wedding; it was the unification of two equals that deserved patience.

Panya peeked at the events from her window. Her attendants laughed and sang as they adjusted her gown. Her anxious eyes focused on the grey clouds gathering in the sky. Clouds were common for the coming season, but for Panya they were a sign of her salvation. Oya would come, of this she was certain. There would be no wedding. Once the rain began she would announce her contact with the orisha and relay her disapproval. If her father did not listen, then Oya would strike him or her groom dead. It didn't make Panya any difference which her patron chose.

Oba Jumoke finally gave the order to open the gates. The wedding party danced in followed by the groom and his entourage. In a normal wedding the groom would be accompanied by his lifelong friends. Instead the Oba of Yubaland, Ladipo Ajose, came accompanied by his court. The nobles entered first, one hundred stern faced men draped in rich blue fabric and gold studded capes. They streamed into Oyo before the enormous train of bride wealth. Six wagons lead them, each filled with the traditional offerings; kola nuts, bitter kola, yams, alligator pepper, honey, pink snapper fish and kente cloth. A herd of goats followed. Behind the goats trailed offerings designed to display Oba Ajose's power. Fifty horses pranced, laden with jeweled harnesses and gilded saddles. Behind them filed one hundred servants holding thick staffs of pure gold crowned with leopard figurines. Ladipo and his attendants followed were the last to enter. The oba of the Yuba rode a white stallion swathed in red fabric and golden plates. His personal guard marched on either side, their dress similar to the mounts. The procession split as it approached Panya's parents, making way for Ladipo.

Panya was oblivious to the ceremony. Her eyes were locked on the gathering clouds.

"Oya, where are you?" she whispered. She was answered by her friend Ebun.

"Come Panya," she said excitedly. "It's time."

Wedding drums echoed throughout the compound as Panya's attendants danced into the courtyard. Panya sauntered in behind them, her face covered. He looked at Ladipo and for the first time felt uncertainty seep into her mind. The oba was not as old as he expected; in fact, he was quite handsome. His smile seemed genuine as she approached, but it did not change the fact that she did not know this man. She sat on her father's lap and the wedding party prayed for the well-being of the marriage. Panya kissed her mother and father then approached Ladipo's family. She kneeled before them and they prayed. Panya sauntered to Ladipo and sat beside him. Her eyes lifted upward but the sky had not changed.

Her father stood and the courtyard fell silent. He looked upon Panya and Ladipo and a victorious smile ruled his face. His expression triggered a spark of anger in Panya and her face warmed. As he turned to face Ladipo's parents, reality dragged down Panya's hope. Oya had abandoned her.

"This is a special day, a special day, indeed," her father began. "The bride and groom sitting before you today represent a host of unions. They are a union of man and woman, a union of families, of spirits, and of kingdoms. When Oba Ladipo first asked for my daughter's hand, I was skeptical to say the least. Oyo and Yubaland are at sometimes enemies, at other times adversaries, but at no time friends. But the world changes and so must men. So I agreed to Ladipo's proposal, for only a fool can hate his family. By this union Oyo and Yubaland become not only united kingdoms, but family. This is a day that the ancestors witness and praise."

Drummers flailed, bells rang, singers sang and dancers danced to punctuate her father's words. Panya glared at her father, heat coursing from her cheeks to her arms. The clouds darkened as they clustered over the wedding party.

It was Ladipo's father time to speak. Malomo Ajose leaned hard on his staff as he stood. The elderly man took his time, tipping to the neutral ground between both families. His face was set hard in a frown; he moved his head slowly from side to side, his wrinkled brow twitching. Panya could sense he was not happy with this marriage but she knew he would not protest. His time as Oba was long past. He could do nothing but acquiesce. Malomo cleared his throat and the courtyard fell silent again.

"I speak for my son, Oba Ladipo. This marriage carries a heavy weight. We all know the history between our people, though no one knows it better than I. The blood of Oyo had stained my sword many times. The women of Yubaland have cried into the night because their men would not return from Oyo's forests. Both kingdoms have homes with bodies underneath because of our wars. But today such times come to an end. Today my son has been granted a gift more precious than gold. Today my son receives not only a beautiful and worthy wife; he also receives peace."

Panya's mother stood as Malomo walked away, her destination the bride wealth.

"Come, Panya," she urged. "Show us what among these gifts is most valuable to you."

Panya rose to her feet and walked absently to her mother's side. She found the Oracle among the gifts, a thick golden ring crowned with amber resting atop it. Every step back to her seat beside Ladipo seemed an eternity. She cursed him silently; she cursed her father, her mother and even Oyewole. Most of all she cursed Oya.

She stood before Ladipo. He took the ring with his thick fingers and placed in on her trembling finger. It was done. She was Ladipo's wife. Her father arranged it and her mother condoned it. Worst of all, Oya permitted it. She was led to Ladipo's mother and they danced. Her mother danced with Ladipo, both of them smiling as if this was a happy day. They danced close to Panya and Ladipo suddenly lifted her off her feet.

"What have you done?" the wedding party shouted.

"I carried the bride!" Ladipo shouted back.

Drums erupted into a celebration rhythm, masking the thunder rumbling overhead. Panya barely noticed the raucous reception. She smiled when she should and spoke kind words to those who spoke to her. Her father mingled proudly among the guests and her mother sat demurely at the table, receiving blessings and gifts. She looked to the other side of the courtyard and saw Oyewole staring back at her. Only he seemed to know how she felt. His face was as grim as she felt inside, his eyes sparkling with tears.

One of his friends placed a friendly hand on his shoulder and he shoved him away. Their other friends grabbed both men and hustled them away, the revelers looking on the commotion curiously. Oyewole looked at her one last time, his expression sympathetic.

Rain splattered on the table before her. The revelers continued to dance, a few looking up nervously at the darkening clouds. Lightning flashed and thunder pounded down on them. The clouds finally unleashed its contents on Oyo. Servants hurried to gather the gifts and food while the other mounted their horses and wagons. Panya did not move; she welcomed the downpour that hid her tears. Oya did not save her but she cried for her.

Panya felt hands grip her wet shoulders and pull her to her feet. She pivoted and looked into her mother's proud eyes.

"You symbolize our people among them," she said. "Represent us well. Be a good wife and our people will always be allies. A wife who controls her husband controls his kingdom."

She hugged Panya and kissed her cheek. Panya's servants pulled her away, rushing her to a white horse cloaked in red kapok. She mounted, took a long look at her home then galloped away with her new family. The wedding party rode for a week through the persistent rain, the constant drenching quickly damping the significance of the ceremony. Ladipo and Panya were kept separate despite them being wed. Panya was kept company by her friends. They would stay with her for one month as she acclimated to her new family. Panya spoke little during the entire journey as she vacillated between anger and fear.

They entered Yubaland under thin grey skies, the rains relenting long enough for Panya to get a good look at her new home. It was a sparse land compared to Oyo; the trees spread apart, shrubs and grasses covering the ground between them. The walls of Bose peeked through the scattered bush, the dark stone in stark contrast to Oyo's white palisades. Warning drums echoed from the ramparts and were quickly answered by the rapid patter of the oba's vanguard drummers. The Yuba sang, reviving the spirit of the wedding ceremony. They were answered by the citizens of the city crowding the rampart to see the arrival of their new queen. The massive iron gates swung wide to reveal a city in full celebration despite the constant drizzle. Bose's magnificence stole Panya's attention from her plight. The city was much larger than Oyo and obviously wealthier. Every house was a stone structure, the doors elaborately carved with images of various animals. A second wall loomed before them, a structure made of a simmering green stone she did not recognize. A pair of metal gates that gleamed like gold parted to a compound more extravagant. The residents were equally profligate. The women were bedecked with jewels and amber that hid the tops of their long bright dresses. The men posed beside their wives in matching pants and shirts, gilded scabbards holding ivory hilted swords dangling from their beaded belts. They bowed as she passed, lifting their heads slightly to see her. Minutes later the party approached another wall, the most extravagant and heavily guarded of the three. Behind it was the compound of the oba, the home of the Ladipo family. It would soon be her home, but to Panya the gilded gates before her may as well been the entrance to a prison.

Lightning cracked overhead and anger surged through her. Two female servants approached her mount, their attention divided between their duty and the threatening sky above. One of the servants grasped the horse's bridle as the other approached her, a nervous smile on her face.

"Welcome to Bose, my queen," she stammered. "I am Chinaza. This is Abiba. We have come to take you to your home and prepare you for the Oba."

Panya did not answer. She was so distraught she'd forgotten that their marriage was to be consummated this night. She said nothing as the servants led her into the compound to a house larger than her father's palace. Abiba knelt beside the horse, offering her back as a stepping stool. Panya avoided her, dismounting with the ease of a person experienced in riding.

"Never do that again," she said. She tramped through the mud and into the house. Once inside she turned to find her friends. They were gone.

She glared at Chinaza. " Where are my sisters?"

Chinaza cleared her throat. "Your sisters were taken to place suitable to their station. Abiba and I will prepare you."

Panya refused to move. She was tired of being told what to do.

Chinaza held out her hand. "Please, my queen. We do what we were commanded to do. Oba Ladipo will punish us if we do not complete our task."

The sky rumbled as Panya reluctantly took Chinaza's hand and followed the servant to the rear of the home. There the women set about their work, delicately undressing Panya then bathing her with coarse soaps. They patted her dry with soft cotton towels then massaged her with Shea butter and soothing, aromatic oils. They covered her in a sheer cotton gown embroidered with gold thread. Panya did not protest. The servants were performing a task; there was no need to waste emotion on them. Abiba fetched a stool and placed it before her.

"Please sit, my queen. We must tend to your hair."

They fussed over her hair as they did her body, washing away the road dust and braiding it into dazzling rows highlighted by gold thread and white beads. Chinaza draped a simple amber necklace on her shoulders then both women stepped away.

Chinaza stepped back and smiled. "We are finished. Is there anything else you require?"

"No." Panya's anger was evident in her voice.

"Then we will leave you," Chinaza announced. The women bowed then scurried away.

Panya was still sitting on the stool when Ladipo entered. His garments were barely wet; he apparently took time to change before coming to her. The smile on his face angered her.

"Chinaza and Abiba have done well. You look beautiful, although it did not take their efforts to make you so."

He stepped toward her and she stepped away. Ladipo's smile faded.

"I know this marriage was not your choice. It never is. We who are chosen must live our lives as we need to, not as we want to. If you wish more time then I will give it."

"I'll never change my mind," Panya said.

Ladipo's smile returned with a different intent. "Then there is no need for me to wait."

Lapido grabbed Panya's wrist and snatched her up from the stool. She jerked back instinctively but Ladipo's grip was strong. A moment of panic was replaced by Oyewole's words.

"Remember what I taught you."

Ladipo jerked her again and Panya leaped toward him, smashing her elbow into his nose and driving her knee into his stomach. Ladipo yelped and staggered back holding his bloodied nose. He leered over his bloodied fingers.

"I see you've been taught to fight. I suspect this is your brother's doing. Let's see what you truly know."

Ladipo sprang like a great cat. Panya jumped aside but not fast enough. His open hand smacked her jaw, spinning her to the floor. His hands gripped her neck as he lifted her to her feet.

"I don't know what you were thinking," he growled. "You are mine. You will do as I say!"

Lightning exploded around them. Thunder battered the roof like the hands of a giant. Panya's body coursed with anxious energy and she smiled like a child. Oya had come. She gripped Ladipo's wrists and twisted. Ladipo struggled to keep his grasp then suddenly let go. "Witch!" he shouted. Panya answered with the kick into his stomach. Ladipo doubled over and she drove her elbow into his back. He fell on his face and Panya jumped onto his back. Oya sat on her head and Panya gave way to the angry goddess. She beat her fists into his head until her hands ran red with his blood and hers. Panya stood, a regal satisfaction burning inside. Who was he to think he could possess her? A feeble man with a weak kingdom, that's what he was. His patch of land was nothing compared to what she owned. The sky was her realm. The wind answered to her command. The storm battering his city paled compared to her true might. She was a goddess. She was…Panya.

Oya left as swiftly as she had come. Panya tottered, her vision blurred. Her eyes cleared and she gazed at Ladipo's body, blood pouring from the back of his head.

"No, no, no!" She looked at her red hands and her shoulders slumped in despair. She ran into the rain and looked into the black sky. Raindrops splattered on her face.

"I did not want this! I only wanted to be free. I only wanted to go home!"

Oya answered with a chorus of deafening thunder and continuous lightning.

"You chose me and I have come. You are my daughter."

Panya slumped into the mud. The rain soaked her gown, plastering it against her skin.

"I can't go home, not after this." She looked up into the sky again. "Where do I go? What do I do?"

The rain slackened about her then ceased.

"I will show you."

Panya stood and the rain slackened. She slogged toward the gates through a gauntlet of rain and lightning forming a barrier between her and the curious Yubabu. A shout rose over the rumbling and Panya flinched. Ladipo's body had apparently been discovered. The crowd outside Oya's barrier bristled with angry warriors, the lightning illuminating their expressions. A group of them attempted to charge her and were immediately struck by lightning. Panya did not look at them. Oya would protect her, but would she protect Oyo? Would she embrace Oyewole, mamma and baba?

"YOU are my daughter."

She followed the gauntlet out of Bose. She was free of the prison behind her but could not return to the prison before her. Her only way was that which Oya showed her.

Panya looked into the drenching darkness before her, the path laid out by Oya. She was Oya's daughter now. She had made her choice.

HEKALU YA MWANGAZA (THE TEMPLE OF LIGHT)

Market day in Mombasa brought the usual crowds to the city center, a discordant mix of buyers and sellers eager to fill their cupboards and coffers. It was also one of the few days that the various folks of the merchant city mixed without distinction, searching the colorful kiosks for life's essentials. Even among the variety of folk, one man stood out. He strode through the throng carrying two sacks of grain on his massive shoulders, a burden that would have bowed the average man. The brown leather vest he wore gripped his broad muscled torso; his cotton pants fit his legs like an extra layer of skin. He bore no sword or knife, but even one whose wits were sparse knew better that to approach him lightly. His presence spoke of a man capable of inflicting damage if need be.

Changa Diop reveled in the freedom of the market. He gazed upon the crowd with joy, ignoring the astonished stares as he made his way back to the dock. It was his third trip to the market that day and each excursion filled him with as much excitement as the first. He was free again, walking among folks without the burden of ownership weighing on his shoulders like the bags of grain he carried. There were still obligations, but they were decisions he made, not those made for him. The horror of the pit was behind him now, but danger still haunted him. Some things were persistent.

That thought alerted Changa that he was being watched. He kept his aloof expression as his eyes probed the swirling mob of the market. He eventually found the source of scrutiny, a tall woman who made no effort to hide her interest. Her head was immodestly bare, revealing her close-cropped hair. She strode through the crowd covered in a black cloak that fell from her shoulders to her ankles. Her face reminded Changa of the Nuba, black smooth skin encompassing a beautiful yet stern face. Changa stared back and smiled; the woman's expression remained unchanged. She halted, watching him as he walked away then melded into the crowd.

By the time Changa reached the docks the woman was but a pleasant memory. His new companions, Belay's *baharia,* waved to him as he approached the dhows. All were smiles except one small boy who stood with his fist planted on his sides, his eyebrows bunched and his small mouth set in a frown.

"Where have you been, Changa?" Tayari asked. Kasim, Belay's nahoda, had assigned his son the task of teaching Changa how to tie good knots. The boy took his job seriously, and was not pleased that Changa didn't share his view.

"I had work to do," Changa answered. "You want to eat, don't you?"

Tayari continued to stare at Changa so intensely that Changa laughed. "Okay, *mwalimu*. I'll set these down and we can continue our lessons."

Changa spent the next hour with Tayari practicing the various knots required for the riggings and other tasks on the dhow. Some were simple and others complex, but Changa had no problem following the boy's swift hands. Afterwards he joined the crew with their chores. He had yet to make any friends among them but at least they were friendlier than his former circumstances. For the first time in years he could fully extend his friendship to others. Unlike the pit, he didn't have to worry about facing any of these men later in a battle to the death.

Night eased across Mombasa, bringing a cool wind from beyond the horizon. Changa lay on the deck, gazing into the star laden sky. He refused to sleep inside except when the rains forced him to. His life in the pit cells continued to influence him despite being so far away.

Sleep was laying its peaceful veil over his eyes when Tayari shook him back to consciousness.

"Changa, Bwana Belay wishes to see you right away," the boy informed him.

Changa dragged himself to a sitting position then stood. "Lead the way," he grumbled.

Tayari led Changa to Belay's home in the center of town. The guard opened the gate to Belay's courtyard, eyeing both Tayari and Changa closely as they entered. Changa stopped suddenly as soon as he entered. Belay sat in his chair, a look of terror on his face. Before him stood the woman Changa saw in the market, the same scrutiniz-ing look on her stern face. A third person stood with them, a man Changa did not recognize physically but he knew by heart. He stood a foot taller than Changa and seemed to weigh twice as much. His bulk was not that of a com-placent merchant; hard muscles pushed against the cotton shirt and pants he wore. A black robe similar to the one the woman wore hung from his massive shoulders with a hood covering his head. The man's attention was focused on Belay.

"What is this?" Changa demanded.

"Silence, *mtwana*," the man rumbled. There was a tone in his voice that demanded obedience; Changa ignored him.

"What is going on, bwana?" Changa asked. "Who are these people?"

The man looked up at Changa. His eyes burned with a malevolent light, hinting of something deeper than evil. Changa had seen such a look only once in his life from a man whose evil took the life of his father.

"Is this the one?" the man said.

The woman nodded. "He's the one."

Changa stepped towards the man and the woman stepped between them. Her hand disappeared into her cloak.

"Changa, stop!" Belay said. "You have no business with him, Dambudso."

"Quiet, merchantman," Dambudso said. "Shamsa said he's who I want. Her judgment is infallible."

"He is not my mtwana," Belay said. "He is a free man."

Dambudso looked Changa up and down. "He has the look of one. It doesn't matter. You owe me, merchant man. Our debt is erased if this man comes with me. If not, there is nothing you can give me that will erase it."

"What do you want of me?" Changa asked.

"Changa, no!" Belay yelled. "This has nothing to do with you."

"As you said, I'm a free man bwana," Changa said. "This is not my business but it's my decision."

Dambudso grinned, an expression that did nothing to make him look more agreeable.

"What do you want?" Changa asked again.

Dambudso approached Changa then stood before him. "I'm taking a journey and I need special men to accompany me. Shamsa tells me you are a special man."

"Where are we going?" Changa asked.

Dambudso's grin became a smile. "A sacred place. There is something there I wish."

"How long will we be gone?"

"Long enough."

Changa looked at Belay. "Will Belay's debt be absolved when you get your something?"

Dambudso nodded. "Of course."

"I'll get my things," Changa said.

"You don't need anything," Dambudso said. "I'll supply you with everything you'll need for the journey."

The mysterious man took one last look at Belay. "Consider you debts paid."

Dambudso strode for the door, Shamsa following. Changa followed them out of Belay's house and into the dark streets of Mombasa. He was taking a risk going with these two but he would not allow Belay to be in danger. The man had bought his freedom and saved his life; it was time for him to return the favor.

The mysterious duo walked through Mombasa's dark streets with no torch, but they moved as if the sun shone overhead. Changa stayed close to them; his eyesight wasn't nearly as keen in such darkness. They halted at the end of the road just before it entered the surrounding farm-land. A wagon rested at the end of the road. Two oxen were hitched to it; an extremely tall man with facial scars sat behind the reins. Two saddled horses flanked the oxen. Men sat in the bed of the wagon, their faces hidden by hoods attached to cloaks similar to Dambudso.

"Put this on and climb in back," Shamsa ordered. In her hand she held a black cloak.

Changa looked at the cloth skeptically. He was well aware of the ways of shaman and was not in the mood to be spellbound.

"You gave your word to Belay that you would do as I ask," Dambudso said. "Are you not a man of your word, Changa?"

Changa snatched the robe from Shamsa's hand and donned it. Immediately he felt refreshed. The inkling of hunger that teased him dissipated. His eyes fell on Shamsa and she smiled.

"It will nourish you during our journey. This way we won't have to waste time finding and eating food."

"I assume this task will require weapons?" Changa asked.

"You will get them when the time comes," Dambudso said. "Unlike you, some of your companions are not very trustworthy."

Changa climbed into the wagon and his new cohorts reluctantly made room for him. They looked up at him, some nodding while others stared. One man finally spoke, uttering a name Changa recently relinquished.

"Mbogo." The man removed his hood and Changa grimaced.

"Katafwa," Changa replied. Both men locked stares, Changa frowning, Katafwa flashing a grim smile.

"I thought I killed you," Changa said.

"You almost did," Katafwa replied. "But no man can kill Death."

"Be quiet!" Dambudso ordered. "From now until we retrieve the Light from the Temple you belong to me. You will obey my every word."

"And if we don't?" Katafwa asked.

Dambudso appeared suddenly beside the wagon. His thick arm shot out like a serpent and his massive hand clutched Katafwa's throat before he lifted the man like a leaf.

"I cannot kill you because I need you," Dambudso hissed. "But there are things worse than your namesake, mtwana."

Dambudso dropped Katafwa into the wagon. The others laughed as Dambudso walked away and mounted his horse. Katafwa rubbed his neck. Changa said nothing, watching Katafwa with mild admiration.

"He's strong," Katafwa said. "Too strong to kill without weapons."

Changa didn't reply. He watched Dambudso and Shamsa mount their horses.

"Let's go, Luk," Dambudso said the Dinka wagon driver. "We have a long journey ahead. I'm anxious to be done with this."

Changa expected a leisurely pace which would allow him to sleep. Instead the riders took off at full gallop. The Dinka did not follow. He sat still and began to sing, his voice low and insistent. The oxen crooned back, their bellows strong and agitated. And then they ran, darting off with a suddenness that caused everyone in the wagon to tumble into each other. Changa flung out his right hand and grasped the edge of the wagon. He pulled himself against it as the Dinka sang louder, his strange melodic voice rising over the rattling wagon. The jostling subsided then ceased. Changa peered over the side and his eyes widened in astonishment. The wagon drifted over the ground, the wheels perfectly still. He looked at the oxen; their legs moved as if they ran across flat ground, but instead their hooves touched nothing. Changa raised his eyes and looked farther ahead. Though Dambudso and Shamsa were dim shapes in the distance, he could tell their mounts travelled the same as the wagon.

"This is Dambudso's work," Katafwa said.

Changa looked to see the man sitting beside him still rubbing his neck. "We will not survive this task. They are speeding us to our death."

Changa didn't reply. He glared at Katafwa, remembering why he disliked the burly Nuba.

"I say we become friends if we want to survive this sentence," Katafwa continued.

His words forced a laugh from Changa's lips.

"Dambudso must have damaged your brain," he said.

"I'm not fond of the idea either, boy," Katafwa countered. "You almost killed me. But I know you better than that bundle over there. I trust your skills."

Changa glanced at the other men in the wagon. It was four of them and they whispered among themselves. It was obvious they knew each other well. As much as he hated to admit it Katafwa's words made sense.

"Who are they?" Changa asked.

Katafwa shrugged. "Who care? They're *mtwana*, just like us."

"Like you," Changa corrected him.

Katafwa's eyebrows rose. "Maulani freed you?"

"No," Changa replied.

Katafwa nodded. "I didn't think so. You made too much money for him."

Changa didn't owe Katafwa an explanation but felt compelled to clarify his status.

"A merchant from Mombasa named Belay bought me from Maulani and freed me soon afterwards," he explained. "He offered me employment as his bodyguard and I accepted."

"So why are you here? As a free man you have no obligation to him. Whatever business he has with that devil Dambudso is his own." Katafwa's eyebrows rose. "Are you his lover?"

Changa glared at Katafwa. "No."

The man shrugged. "Don't look at me like that. Many a pious Swahili are only so among each other. Once in their stone houses a different master reigns."

"I owe him," Changa answered. "He freed me."

Katafwa laughed out loud and the other men looked in their direction.

"Mbogo is a man with a conscience!" He leaned close to Changa, his hot breath annoying the BaKonga. "Take my advice and lose it as soon as you can. It will be the death of you."

"Seems it already has," Changa said.

The two reluctant cohorts remained silent the rest of the night, Changa wondering where their mysterious journey would end. The wagon's journey resembled that of a dhow, smooth yet undulating as if it rode gentle waves. Daybreak eventually emerged behind him; the sun's light creeping over the stunted treetops. Changa had traveled beyond Mombasa a number of times but never had he seen landscape like that which became clear in the growing sunlight. It was neither thick forest nor open savannah. It was barren like a desert, yet even the desert was not as barren as the land stretching out before them. Signs of former life surrounded them; grey trees with empty branches resembling extended bones, bleached skeletons of creatures Changa knew well and others he didn't recognize at all. Whatever had reduced this land to waste was not natural. The wagon jolted, acquiring the normal cadence of a wagon connected to the ground. The Dinka ceased singing and his oxen responded with a short bellow. They halted, surrounded by the unnatural nothingness. Shamsa and her mount sauntered to the wagon, the woman's face still grim.

"We will rest here," she said. The oxen need nourishment. Don't take off your robes until we reach the temple grounds."

"There is a temple in this waste?" Katafwa asked.

Changa didn't think Shamsa's expression could get grimmer but it did.

"You talk too much," she said. "Just do as I say."

Her piercing eyes fell on Changa. "You, walk with me."

She reined her horse about and began to ride away. Changa hesitated, unsure of the woman's intentions. She stopped then looked over her shoulder expectantly. Changa climbed from the wagon and followed.

"We go to retrieve an object very important to Dambudso," she said. "It is an object of extreme value to him."

"Dambudso appears to be a man of great power," Changa said. "I'm puzzled that he would need our help...and yours."

Shamsa looked at him, and Changa thought he almost saw her smile.

"Under normal circumstances you would be right," she answered. "But everyone has a weakness. Dambudso needs you and the others to get near his prize. He needs me to retrieve it."

"And what is your debt to him?" Changa asked.

"I owe him no debt," she said. "I owe him a favor."

"Katafwa says we'll all die," Changa said. "Is that true?"

Shamsa sucked her teeth. "Katafwa talks too much. It was a mistake bringing him."

"You haven't answered my question," Changa reminded her.

"It's likely you will," she admitted. "But you have a chance to survive."

Changa's mood brightened. "How?"

"Stay close to me and do everything I say," she said. "Go back to your friends and say nothing of our conversation."

Changa nodded and returned to the wagon. The Dinka had placed a blanket made of the same material as his robe over the oxen. He sat before them in his own robe that swirled with colors and symbols. He hummed as he stroked the beasts' muzzles, oblivious to the barren land around him. Changa climbed back into the wagon. No sooner had he sat did Katafwa scoot beside him.

"So what secrets did the stone princess share with you?" he asked eagerly. "And why did she share them only with you?"

"She seems to think I can help her," Changa answered.

"With what?"

"I don't know."

"Keep your distance, Mbogo," Katafwa advised. "Trust no one."

"You seem to be full of wisdom," Changa replied, "yet you sit here just as vulnerable as I. Why are you here?"

Katafwa shrugged. "I am a mtwana. I had no choice."

"You don't seem like the kind of man who would agree easily to such a task."

"I was the best choice," Katafwa said. "My mistress's other mtwanas are domestic help. I am her only fighter."

"You're not much of one," Changa replied.

"With my hands, no," Katafwa admitted. "But give me a spear or a sword and the meaning of my name becomes very clear."

"So, you are your mistress's shield," Changa commented.

A solemn look came over Katafwa's face. "I perform other duties as well."

It was Changa's turn to be surprised. "You are her lover?"

"You say that as if it was impossible," Katafwa said with a bitter tone. "Apparently my mistress is one who craves the constant attention of men. When my master died she decided to request that attention from me. She is a lovely woman and I was happy to oblige. But like a fool I fell in love with her. I'm sure the feeling is not mutual for if it was I wouldn't be here. I volunteered thinking she would say no."

"I have never been in love," Changa said.

"You're not missing a thing," Katafwa answered.

Movement on the horizon caught Changa's eye. The border between earth and sky faded into a roiling mass of sand.

"It looks like a sandstorm is coming," Katafwa commented.

"That is no storm," Dambudso said, his voice booming over them all. "It is an attack."

He dismounted his horse and took a thick bundle from behind the saddle. Kneeling beside the wagon, he undid the leather straps holding the bundle tight then rolled it open, revealing eight swords. They were magnificent weapons, the curved blades shining in the dimming light, the pommels carved from ivory and studded with jewels. Katafwa immediately jumped from the wagon and took one of the blades in his hand. He caressed the weapon with his left hand, his eyes wide with wonder.

"Now this is a sword!" His smile was infectious despite the impending danger.

"The rest of you get down here and arm yourselves!" Dambudso barked. "I can kill most of them but not all of them. Hurry!"

Changa and the others climbed out the wagon and chose their swords. Changa was disappointed with the blade. Though pretty, it was lighter than he was used to.

"Don't be deceived," Katafwa said as if reading his mind. "These are Damascus swords. They can withstand the strongest blows yet cut like a razor." Katafwa grabbed the tip of his blade and bent it almost into a U shape.

Changa repeated the gesture. He still wasn't impressed.

Shamsa walked in their midst. "Close you cloaks and pull your hoods completely over your faces. If the sand touches your skin it will tear it away."

"We won't be able to see!" one of the other men argued.

"Do as I say if you want to live, fool!" Shamsa shouted.

Shamsa looked long at Changa before following her own advice. Changa pulled the hood over his face. His sight was obscured but not completely blocked. He stared at the advancing tempest and stiffened as the black mesh revealed the truth behind the storm. Shapes flowed within the sands, some human-like, some not, but all closing rapidly on them. Changa looked at his companions then to Dambudso and Shamsa, the only barrier between him and the coming menace. There was nowhere to run, not that he would. He hoped the sword he held in his hand was as mighty as Katafwa claimed. The Dinka seemed oblivious. He covered his oxen with a black shroud then lay against them, his singing constant and soothing.

Changa watched Dambudso push Shamsa behind him. The shaman stretched out his arms, his shoulders rising and falling in perfect rhythm. Tendrils extended from his fingers, thin wisps so frail it was hard for Changa to determine they truly existed. They grew longer and wider, the air shimmering in their presence. They detached from his hands and expanded more, forming a translucent shell about them. The sandstorm and its creatures assaulted the barrier moments later. While the shield held back the swirling sands it did not stop the beasts hidden within. Two serpent-like creatures leaped out the sand at Dambudso, their maws wide. Shamsa stepped between the shaman and the beasts swinging her blade wide. Green fluid sprayed from them as their heads fell from their bodies and rolled by Shamsa's feet. Changa was so mesmerized by the sudden demise that he almost lost his own life. A bull-like creature smashed its head into Changa's ribs, knocking him into the air like a wind-blown leaf. He landed awkwardly but managed to roll to a kneeling position, his sword raised instinctively. The bull creature was charging him again. Changa waited until it was almost upon him before rolling to his right as he slashed at the side of its thick neck. His blade bit into the strange flesh and he was rewarded by the painful howl of his attacker. Green liquid sprayed into his face, blinding him. Before he could wipe it away something slammed into his back, knocking him forward into the sand. Small sharp hands clawed at him, tearing at his shroud and pulling at his fingers clutching the hilt of his sword. Changa let out a yell and pushed to his feet. He reached back then tore the monkey-like creature from his back, throwing it as far as he could. The creature landed on its hands and feet then attacked again. Changa swung his sword with both hand, cleaving the beast in two.

Sand stung his skin where his shroud had been torn. He took a quick look around and was dismayed. Dambudso still stood like a statue, arms outstretched. Shamsa danced about him, fighting off the various denizen emerging from the abrasive swirl. The other warriors struggled as he had, clawing the sand creatures from their bodies while swinging wildly with their swords. One man's shroud was ripped away and the sand swarmed him like locusts. His screams were drowned out then ceased; when the sand dispersed a skeleton crumbled to the ground. Changa would not lose his shroud.

Another shout caught Changa's attention, although this was not a call of distress. He looked to see Katafwa moving with a grace similar to Shamsa, working his Damascus with a skill far beyond the ordinary. His flashing blade formed a shield around him more effective than the Dambudso's tendrils, creatures piling at his feet in a morbid collection. With each kill Katafwa shouted, yelled or laughed. Katafwa didn't lie to him earlier. He was a master with a sword. Creatures fell before him almost as fast as they fell to Shamsa's blade. It was why Changa stood unmolested; Katafwa's fury drew the attention of the other creatures. Changa took advantage, attacking them from behind. The other warriors offered Katafwa no such assistance. They huddled by the wagon, happy to be free of the onslaught. The creatures responded to Changa's attack and set upon him, but he was prepared. Together he and Katafwa battled the nefarious denizens until the attack trickled away then ceased. Changa looked about; the sand stormed abated and with it the attack. Dambudso slowly lowered his arms as Shamsa kept a focused vigil about him. As the sand cleared Changa and the others were finally able to see the true threat to their lives. Hundreds of creatures lay dead beyond the barrier. He realized that without the shaman's mystical dome they would have been easily overwhelmed.

Dambudso scanned the area then nodded his head. He looked at Shamsa.

"Gather their weapons," he said.

Shamsa immediately complied. He took the weapons from the tribesmen huddled near the wagon, disgust clear on her face. She approached Changa and Katafwa with an expression resembling a smile on her face. Changa handed over his Damascus reluctantly. Katafwa did not.

"This is a fine blade," he said. "Too fine to give up so easily."

"Don't," Shamsa warned.

Katafwa's feet slid apart as he raised the sword. "You can have it if you…"

Katafwa disappeared, replaced by Dambudso's bulk. He held the Damascus in his hand. Glaring at Changa, he absently gave the blade to Shamsa.

"See to your friend," he said. He pointed behind Changa.

Changa turned to see Katafwa sprawled in the sand face down. Changa trotted to the man and rolled him on his back. There was no obvious movement; he leaned closer and felt his breath.

"He's alive," Changa shouted.

"Too bad," Dambudso commented. "I grow weary of him."

Shamsa folded her arms before her, clearly agitated by Dambudso's actions.

"We still need all of them. Besides, he's the best swordsman."

Dambudso shrugged. "His cloak will heal him eventually. Get them in the wagons."

"We must hurry," Shamsa said. "They are preparing for us."

Dambudso glared at her. "Don't state the obvious. Just make sure you are ready to perform your task. I will be very disappointed if you fail."

Changa felt the threat in Dambudso's words as he carried Katafwa to the wagon. Shamsa seemed unaffected.

"I will." She climbed on her steed. "As you said, we are wasting time."

Dambudso mounted his horse as well as the warriors climbed into the wagon. The cohorts looked at the bones of their comrade with sadness and fear. Changa sat beside Katafwa then placed his hand on the man's chest. He was breathing but barely. He did not question the healing abilities of the cloaks but he was concerned if the enchanted shroud would do its job before they reached their mysterious destination. They would need his amazing skills.

The Nuba uncovered his bovine and climbed onto the wagon. He began singing the familiar song and the wagon rose over the sand. Once again, they were streaking across the land at and incredible speed, the sand blurring beneath them. The mountains in the distance were their obvious destination; what secret they held Changa would soon discover.

At least that was what he thought. Despite their speed three days passed and they seemed no closer to their destination. The mountains slowly grew in stature until they could no longer see their snow-capped peaks. Changa was no stranger to mountains. His homeland was dotted with verdant peaks, but none were as massive as those looming before them.

"Damn it."

Changa looked down into Katafwa's disappointed eyes.

"Welcome back," he said.

Katafwa struggled to sit up. "It seems my plan failed."

"What plan?" Changa asked.

"I should be dead," Katafwa said. "I was sure those sand things would kill be, but I guess I overestimated their ferocity."

"So you chose Dambudso."

Katafwa winced and touched his chest where the wizard slammed into him.

"Yes I did. I figured since he almost killed me before he would be happy to finish the job."

Changa smirked. "He almost did. You can thank your cloak that you sit among us."

Katafwa grimaced. "I'd rather sit among my ancestors."

Katafwa's eyes scanned the wagon. "We are missing one."

Changa controlled a shudder. "The sand consumed him. I saw it."

"Better you than me," Katafwa said. "Maybe we'll all be consumed by something before this is all over."

Changa refused to let Katafwa's morbid musing enter his head. He looked ahead; the mountains now appeared as a massive stone wall before them. Details became clear, thick wasted trees with canopies resembling mushroom caps towered over smaller twisted brethren while the spaces between them was thick with shrubs. Changa could make out some sort of a road through the dense foliage. He traced it up the mountain until his eyes focused on the entrance to a massive temple. The building was too large to be built by men alone he was sure. This was a structure assembled by the type of power Dambudso possessed.

The massive magic man suddenly reined his horse. Shamsa did the same. The Nuba's melodic coaxing ended with an abrupt command and the oxen ceased their levitated run. The wagon eased to the ground. Dambudso dismounted and marched to the wagon.

"Get out, all of you," he said, his eyes locked on Katafwa. Changa and the other clambered out to the wagon. Shamsa rode up to them, dismounted then distributed the weapons.

"You will follow Shamsa to the temple," Dambudso said, gesturing without looking. "You will obey her every command. If you return you and your masters will be richly rewarded."

Katafwa folded his arms across his chest then tilted his head to the side.

"And what will you do?" he asked.

Changa waited for Dambudso to strike, but he did not. Instead a frustrated look commanded his face.

"I will stay here," he said.

Katafwa's eyes widened and he grinned. "And why is that, great mage?"

Changa grabbed Katafwa's arm. "Be quiet!"

Dambudso grimaced before dropping his head. "Because I can go no further."

Shamsa strode to the both of them and shoved Katafwa.

"Be quiet, fool! You live on my grace only. Remove your cloaks and follow me."

For the first time since their journey began one of the secretive warriors spoke.

"Why? Won't they protect us?"

Shamsa glared at him. "Not anymore."

The cohorts looked about fearfully. Katafwa was the first to follow. Changa followed, looking back at the others. The cohort finally fell in step.

Changa worked his way close to the warrior woman. "Why is it that Dambudso cannot come with us?"

Shamsa pointed at the temple. "That is the Temple of Light. Once it was the symbol of faith for all those who lived in its shadow. The priests of the Temple performed wonderful things and the lands prospered. But one of those priests was more talented than the others. He grew to high status, so much so that he began to think he was equal to his gods. The day came that he called the people to the temple steps and proclaimed himself a living god. He told the people they would worship and sacrifice to him from that day forth."

"Dambudso," Katafwa said.

"What happened?" Changa asked.

Shamsa's eyes narrowed. "He was punished."

They reached the base of the mountain. Changa sensed a change in the energy surrounding him. A sense of foreboding crept into his mind, a feeling that what they were doing was terribly wrong. He looked at the others; the cohorts shivered despite the humid heat. Only Shamsa and Katafwa seemed unaffected, Shamsa's face locked in her familiar frown and Katafwa smiling like a child. Shamsa stepped into the bush, following the road into the heights. Changa close behind her. The sensation grew the higher they climbed.

"No!" Changa turned to look behind him. The cohorts stood still, the four holding their weapons threateningly.

"We will not go any further!" Their spokesman was the tallest of the three, a man whose scared face told that he was a man familiar with conflict.

"We came to pay a debt for our masters," he complained. "We did not come to die!"

Shamsa pushed Changa aside, stomping down to confront the three.

"You mean nothing to your masters," she hissed. "That's why you are here. They don't care if you live or die and neither do I. All that matters to them is that their debt is paid. All that matters to me is that you walk up this hill and do as you are told. Either you follow me up this hill or you die here. Your choice."

The man's fear faded from his eyes, replaced by fury. "I will not…"

Shamsa's arm flashed. The man's head jumped from his neck and disappeared into the close bush. His body stood before her for a moment, blood oozing from his neck, then collapsed at Shamsa's feet. She reached down with her left hand, lifting the man's body like a child's then tossing it into the bush.

"Either you follow me or you die here," she repeated.

The others glanced at the bush where their cohort lay. They sheathed their weapons and lowered their heads in submission. Shamsa wiped her blade and strode back to the front.

"Katafwa, take position behind them. If they try to flee, kill them."

"Of course," Katafwa answered.

Shamsa continued up the trail, Changa following close.

"You have a problem with my actions, Changa?" she asked without turning to look at him.

"They will not fight for you," he answered, his foreboding replaced by anger.

"I don't need them to fight for me. I just need them to fight."

Shamsa stopped and raised her hand. They had reached the edge of the bush. Before them was an open area strewn with fallen timber and other debris. In the center of the ragged field the temple stood. The structure was more massive that it appeared from the distance, a granite monument draped with thick vines except at the towering entrance. A pulsing light shone from the aperture.

"What happened?" Changa whispered.

"Dambudso was not the only one punished for his arrogance. Those who chose to worship him were punished, too."

"They were killed?"

Shamsa looked at Changa with a mix of annoyance and worry. "Some of them. The others are waiting for us."

Shamsa strode into the open. Changa and Katafwa followed immediately but the cohorts hesitated. Their eyes darted back and forth, scanning the edge of the clearing. A quick backward glance by Shamsa ended their resistance; they crept into the clearing and made their way to the temple.

Again, size distorted distance. The trek to the temple was much longer than Changa anticipated. The temple grew higher and higher, finally reaching the height where looking at the top caused him to lean his head back far enough to strain his neck. The staircase before them was as wide as a main avenue in Mombasa, fully capable to hold five ox carts side by side. They towered to a landing beyond their sight. Again, Shamsa did not hesitate, attacking the stairs with impatience, her scowl depending with each step. Again, Changa and Katafwa followed.

Close to the landing a strange sound reached their ears. Shamsa stopped, crouching low with her sword in guard position. She looked at Changa and Katafwa.

"Once we reach the landing our task will begin. Fight with all you have and stay close to me. I will need you."

Shamsa sprang forward, leaping over the last five steps. Changa ran forward as fast as he could, but Katafwa sprinted by him. Changa caught the same crazed look that Katafwa held when he fought the sand demons. When Changa reached the landing Shamsa was charging across the stone floor. Warriors converged on her, large armored men bearing lances leveled at her. Changa reached at his side then cursed; he had no throwing knives for Dambudso did not think to provide him with any. He soon saw that his intervention was not needed. Shamsa leaped high over the lances then came down slashing. Blood spurted from the throats of the two before her feet touch the stone. By the time the other warriors reached her Changa and Katafwa were by her side.

Changa had no time to prepare himself. A guardian fell on him immediately, wielding his lance like an extension of himself. Changa struggled to match his speed, the blade nicking his flesh with each thrust and slash. He ducked a swing at his neck then kicked at the relentless man's leg. His foot met the shaft of the lance, but his sword found the man's torso, piercing his hardened leather armor. No sooner did he fall away that he was replaced by another warrior. Changa focused on the fight before him now. He moved with the speed and power of a leopard, dodging, parrying and cutting his way through the endless on-slaught of armored foe. Occasionally a hearty laugh would rise over the din of ringing steel and grunts, letting Changa know that Katafwa was still alive. For a moment no one stood before him; he scanned the situation and was not encouraged. Shamsa was surrounded by warriors; Katafwa fought his way toward her, his face locked in a crazed grin. The cohorts were dead, their bodies strewn at the edge of the landing. Changa ran to one of them and pried a sword from the dead man's grip.

He fell into the rear of the horde surrounding on Shamsa, both swords flailing. Together he and Katafwa cut her free, although once with her they realized their help was not needed. Temple guard swords had not held her at bay, only their numbers and mass had blocked her from her goal. With them slain there was nothing standing between the three and the innards of the temple.

A blinding light pulsed at the end the column bordered corridor, an illumination so bright Changa turned away, shielding his eyes. No sooner that he'd done so did the light begin to dim.

"No!" Shamsa shouted. She gripped Changa's shoulder, her nails digging into his shoulder and drawing blood.

"We must hurry!" She ran and Changa struggled to keep pace. He glanced backwards; Katafwa was not with them. He stood alone; legs braced far apart, swords in both hands. More warriors swarmed over the lip of the staircase, lances lowered and violent cries in their throats, Changa tried to break free from Shamsa's grip but her fingers dug deeper.

"He will be fine on his own," she snarled. "I need you with me."

Changa glanced back. Katafwa ran at his attackers, his laughter mingling with their battle cries. He could look no more; he needed his energy to keep pace with Shamsa.

When they entered the temple chamber the light had diminished to a glow. The chamber was vast, almost as wide as the clearing they traversed. The granite wall writhed with countless carvings, stark images of men, women and animals contorted in unnatural ways. Their footfalls echoed off the walls as they ran to the opposite side of the chamber. Their objective came into focus with each step. A cavernous hole punctured the granite, an opening filled with a massive carving. A feline head filled the cavern; its mouth gaped open to reveal the light source. Paw-like hands lapped over the edge of the crypt, nails like swords extending from its fingers.

The eerie silence of the chamber was shattered by a deafening rumble. Shamsa stopped running. She turned to Changa, her brow furrowed in frustration.

"We are too late," she said. "But we still have a chance. Take this!"

Shamsa threw Changa her sword. He dropped one of his own, caught the hilt of her blade and immediately regretted it. The metal hilt burned the palm of his hand like fire.

"Don't let it go!" she yelled.

Changa grimaced as he fought to hold the blade. The heat subsided to pulsing warmth. He looked at Shamsa puzzled.

She smiled. "It will not fail you now."

The chamber rumbled again and the floor trembled. Changa's eyes went to the feline face. The light was almost gone, but it was not that fact that caught his notice. The paws that had once rested on the edge of the cavern now touched the ground. The feline had moved.

Shamsa sprinted out of his vision. Changa back pedaled, Shamsa's blade wavering in his tense hands. A constant rumbled vibrated the chamber, the carved images in the wall animated by the disturbance. A searing, grating sound accompanied the rumble as the feline emerged from its narrow chamber, blinking its grey eyes. The light disappeared as the being closed its maw then stood. It was enormous, a wide living being of stone standing the height of twenty men. Changa did the only thing he could do. He ran.

The feline releases a deafening roar. Its footfalls boomed like a drum as it pursued Changa, stone shattering with each step, the floor quaking beneath his sandaled feet. Then the shaking stopped. Changa did not look back; he continued to run for the chamber entrance. Suddenly darkness descended before him. The ground pitched and he flew off his feet then landed on his face. He scrambled back to his feet and stiffened. The stone cat crouched before him, a deep snarl escaping from its clenched teeth.

A paw flashed at him and Changa instinctively raised Shamsa's sword. He expected the blade to fly from his hands but instead it cut into the stone as easily as flesh. The stone cat howled and jerked the paw away. A bolt of confidence shot though Changa; he was not so defenseless after all. Still, he knew he was no match for the massive stone beast. He had to get out of the chamber.

The stone cat stalked toward him, its eyes focused. Changa circled, trying to work his way toward the opening while keeping an eye on the massive beast. He saw movement just beyond his sight; he focused without taking his eyes of the cat. It was Shamsa. She crawled along the figurines in wall, stealthy working her way over the cat beast. Changa waved his sword, partly to keep the beast's attention and partly to let Shamsa know he saw her. She responded by increasing her pace.

The cat suddenly rose onto its hind legs and howled. It dropped with both paws together, hurtling down at Changa. He waited then rolled away. The paws slammed into the floor, punching a hole where Changa once stood. He was about to stand when a paw slapped him. He slid across the floor then slammed into the opposite wall. Dazed and wounded, he scrambled to stand as the cat ran across floor. Changa leaned on the wall, fighting to remain conscious. The cat jumped, paws outstretched and mouth wide. Shamsa appeared on its head and Changa had a glimpse of hope. That hope was dashed and he saw her jump from the feline's head and into its mouth. He had resigned himself to death when Shamsa reappeared. She tumbled from the cat's maw, her body illuminated. She landed under the cat then rolled away. The cat became rigid in mid jump. Its eyes lost the glow of life, its limbs stiffened. It crashed onto the floor and a shower of dust and stone converged on Changa. He fell to the floor into a ball as stone slammed the wall above, around and on him. Changa clenched his teeth, absorbing the battering until it ceased. He lay buried, barely holding on to consciousness. The burden atop him slowly diminished until he felt a warm hand on his back then tug at his shirt.

"Get up," Shamsa said. "We are not done."

Changa stood, dust and stone falling away from his frame. Shamsa was walking away, her path lit by the light taken from the fragmented stone idol. Changa stepped from the rubble and limped after her. He followed her out of the temple to the temple stairs. There he found Katafwa. He lay dead among a pile of temple guardians, swords still clenched in his hands. He'd finally received his wish. He was among the ancestors.

Changa slowly gained on Shamsa as they crossed the temple field. By the time they reached Dambudso Changa stood beside her.

"Give me my sword," she said. Changa handed the charmed blade back to her.

Dambudso's wide eyes were illuminated by the glowing object in Shamsa's hand.

"At last!" he shouted. "The gods now know I cannot be denied. They will taste my vengeance!"

He extended his hands. "Give it to me."

Shamsa nodded, and then plunged her sword into Dambudso's chest. Dambudso's shocked expression faded as life drained from his body. Shamsa extracted her blade as he fell to the ground.

She turned to Changa. Changa stepped away, preparing for her attack. Instead she dropped her sword and began to disrobe.

"At last," she whispered.

Shamsa stood nude before Changa. She gave him a sly smile then slowly pressed the luminous object against her breasts. The temple light disappeared into her chest then slowly spread throughout her body. The features of her face melted away; soon all the remained of the stern woman was her female form. Her blue visage transformed into a red-orange light that emitted heat like a roaring flame. Changa covered his face and staggered away.

"Go home, Changa," she said, her voice ringing inside his head. "Your work is done. Belay's debt is paid.

"What are you?" he asked.

"I have sought a way home for a long time," she answered. "One day I heard of a temple that contained the

Light. I searched in vain until I encountered Dambudso. By that time, I'd developed a certain reputation."

Her radiance grew more intense and Changa shielded his eyes.

"I care little for the beings on this plane, but even I could see that Dambudso was not one to support. But he served his purpose. I have the light; my reward to you was to rid you of such a vile man."

Changa was cowering now, the light and the heat becoming unbearable.

"You have the strength of the spirits inside you Changa. Use it well. I will be watching you."

The being Changa knew as Shamsa slowly rose into the sky. By the time she reached the treetops she was formless light, illuminating the land like a small sun. She lingered for a moment then streaked away into the heavens.

Changa watched her disappear into the wide sky. He stood stunned, attempting to comprehend what had just occurred, then stopped. He was injured but he was alive. He looked about him to get his bearings. The Nuba and his oxen rested patiently, the oxen chewing on the grass, the Nuba singing softly as always. Changa limped to the wagon and looked inside. The cloaks were still there; he took one out and donned it. The healing sensation rushed through him, Dambudso's magic lingering after his death. Changa took another robe from the wagon.

"Do not leave," he said to the Nuba. The man looked at him and nodded. Changa made his way back to the temple. He climbed the temple steps then found Katafwa's body. Wrapping it in a cloak, he lifted him onto his shoulders and descended the steps. He half hoped the cloak would revive his new-found friend but it would not be. When he reached the wagon Katafwa was still dead. His spirit was with the ancestors now. Changa would take him back to the mistress he loved. Maybe she would mourn him and give him the proper burial. If not, Changa would.

He laid Katafwa gently into the wagon then climbed in.

"Take us home," he said.

The Nuba answered by singing loudly. The oxen broke their feast and walked, the wagon rocked gently from side to side as it slowly disappeared into the surrounding forest.

EL SIROCCO

Amenokal Sirocco watched the Bedouin guide lead the caravan towards the oasis from the cover of the dense date palms, his hand gripping the gilded reins of his white camel. This was a large caravan; five hundred camels stretching single file into the horizon burdened by loads of gold, cotton and carved goods from the south destined for the salt markets to the north. But there would be no such rendezvous.

Sirocco twisted in his saddle to face the warriors waiting patiently behind him, raising his hand as he scanned their hard eyes. Some had ridden with him since the beginning, sharing in the spoils of his countless raids. Others were recent volunteers from tribes across the Sahara hoping to be chosen to join his clan. Fears of his cruelty were tempered by the promise of abundance under his rule. Many would die, but most would survive to reap the rewards of the raid. To the people of Tinariwen, Sirocco was more than a man.

Sirocco extracted his scimitar from its sheath then raised it over his head. His commanders raised their takoubas, waiting for his signal. Sirocco looked to the caravan again then grinned. They were in position.

Sirocco sliced the air with his scimitar and his warriors surged into the open. The caravan guard responded in confusion, some riding out to meet the charge, others fleeing for the safety of the surrounding dunes. Sirocco's vanguard, mounted on his swiftest camels, surged ahead, killing the fleeing guide as they charged. The caravan guards that chose to fight met them bravely, their furious defense devolving the charge into a swirling dance of sand, swords and blood. Sirocco plunged into the melee, circling his scimitar over his head. A foolish guard rushed him, his lance lowered for the opening. Sirocco slipped aside and slashed down with both hands gripping the hilt, cutting the man almost in half. His legendary speed was clearly evident as he hacked his way through the confused battle, blocking and parrying his way closer to the prize. As he neared the packed camels five mounted men draped in black emerged from the horde. Sirocco smiled under his shesh; the Askia of Songhai had sent his assassins again, sacrificing a fortune in men and goods to bring his raids to an end. It wasn't the first time the king's bounty hunters had hidden among the merchants, hoping to collect the enormous price on his head. He leaped off his camel and pulled out his second sword, the traditional weapon of the Ihaggaren, the takouba. Swords in both hands, he sauntered towards the assassins.

The assassins dismounted, drew their sabers then attacked. Sirocco blocked a downward stroke as he sidestepped a thrust at his abdomen. He spun, swinging his takouba across the throat of the third man as his scimitar sliced the jaw of the fourth man. He faced the other three as the two wounded men howled in pain. The men attacked in unison, each aiming at a different spot on his body. Sirocco jumped away then dropped to his knees, cutting the three across the shins. He rose as they fell, their swords tumbling from their hands. With three strokes they were dead.

His arm stung and he turned to face the man with the ripped cheek. The man barely stood, his bloody sword held in both hands. Sirocco feinted with his takouba, drawing the man's attention to an overhead blow then slashing his throat with his scimitar. The assassin collapsed to the ground with his comrades.

The battle was done; the caravan folk had been killed to a man. Sirocco strode to his camel, his servants and warriors gathering around him. Usually their eyes were cast down, but they stared at his wounded arm, their eyes wide with disbelief. Sirocco ignored their rudeness. There were others whose reactions concerned him more.

The tribal chiefs waited at the center of the caravan, each surrounded by his own clansmen. The insult was obvious; they remained on their camels as Sirocco and his warriors approach. The cut on his arm was more than a wound; it was a sign of weakness. Never in their life had they seen the blood of El Sirocco spilled in battle.

Sirocco read their thoughts; he decided to get matters over with. He marched into the center of the circle, raised his wounded arm then took out his dagger and cut the sleeve free for everyone to see.

"It is a scratch," he announced.

Aljilani, chief of the Faday clan, urged his camel forward. "It seems more to me."

"Your eyes are weak, brother," Sirocco replied. "Come closer."

Aljilani attacked, his camel galloping at Sirocco. Sirocco sidestepped his charge then snatched an allarh, an iron spear, from one his men. He threw the spear through Aljilani with his wounded arm. The chieftain tumbled from his camel, his eyes frozen in shock. Aljilani's men gathered about him and dragged his body away, respectful fear in their eyes. The men would whisper among themselves that even when wounded El Sirocco was formidable. He was truly the Desert Wind.

The spoils were divided among the clans, the largest portion going to Sirocco. They rode back singing to their kel in the hills, another successful raid to enrich their families. Sirocco was not in a singing mood. He focused on the tents belonging to Aljilani's clan. Aljilani was dead; all that he possessed was forfeit to his slayer. Sirocco's men gathered about him, one hand holding the reins of their camels, the other their allarhs. With a simple nod from him they rushed the cluster of tents, quickly striking down the servants left to protect the chieftain's family. The response was immediate; Aljilani's wife, Leila, charged from her tent to confront them.

"What is the meaning of this?" she demanded, "Why are you doing this?"

Sirocco guided his mount to the woman. "Your husband is dead."

Leila fell to her knees, her eyes glistening. "Who killed him?"

Sirocco smiled. "I did. He challenged me and lost. I've come to claim what is mine and see to his sons."

The women wailed in a morbid chorus as Sirocco's men tore them away from their sons. Sirocco watched, a shred of emotion attempting to break free from deep inside. He remembered the day his father died. The chieftain that slew him rode into camp the same way, intent on claiming his father's wealth and eliminating any chance of revenge. Word had preceded him and the boys were urged to flee. His brothers were too afraid, clinging to their mothers in hopes that the chieftain would accept their allegiance. Sirocco held no such illusions. He took his father's takouba, allarh and ayar, and then fled alone into the desert. It was then he learned of the pain of losing a family. Two days later the camel riders appeared on his trail, warriors sent by the chieftain to kill the last remaining heir. But they had underestimated him. At the age of twelve Sirocco's fighting skills was superior to most men twice his age. The men caught up to him, to their misfortune. On that day Sirocco killed his first men and gained their possessions. Five years later he returned to his kel at the head of his own warriors, killing the man who slew his father and claiming the clan as his own. He knew more than anyone else how important it was to deal with the sons of his adversaries.

He stood over the wailing women, waiting patiently for their sobbing to subside.

"You are my wives now," he declared. "All that was once your husband's is mine."

He turned to the gathering crowd, ignoring the glares and whispers.

"Such is our way," he spoke. "You all have witnessed."

El Sirocco marched back to his tent, his bodyguards following him inside the large enclosure. The interior was bare for a man of his status. Besides his pillows and a few chests holding his clothing and weapons there was little else. The possessions he gained meant nothing to him. Eventually he would let Aljilani's wives find other husbands and begin new families. He had no wives of his own though he never slept alone; the women of his kel frequently slipped into his tent under the stars, eager to pleasure him in hopes of giving birth to a child of his talents. Sirocco cared nothing for any of it. To him it was like the sand, coming and going at the whim of the winds. The only thing of value to him was his life. He surrounded himself with others for a man could not live in the desert alone. He draped himself with charms and talisman to protect him from threats unseen. The cut on his arms told him his charms had failed him.

"Bring me the witch now!" he ordered. He sat cross-legged on his silk pillows, waiting restlessly for the men to return. They entered the tent minutes later with an old woman wearing a patterned dressed and black burka signifying her profession. They shoved the woman to the ground.

The woman spoke in a weak voice without looking up. "What have I done to offend you, master?"

Sirocco snatched the talisman bag from his neck and threw it at the woman.

"You cheated me, Akuji!" he yelled. "This gris-gris is useless!"

Akuji slowly raised her head to look at the bag before her.

"I use the strongest nyama for you, master. The ceremonies of preparation lasted well into the night. The spirits I called upon do not come easily or cheaply."

"So how do you explain this?" Sirocco showed the woman his wound.

"The talisman was prepared to keep you alive," Akuji explained. "The fact that you sit here before me proves its worth."

Sirocco leaped to his feet, sword in hand. The woman yelped and tried to flee, but he was too fast. He beat her with the flat of his blade until the woman barely moved. Sirocco stood over her for a moment then returned to his pillows.

"Dump her beyond the hills," he said. "Maybe there is enough magic left in her pouch to keep the jackals away."

He threw the men a pouch of gold. "Go to the city and find me another witch."

The guards dragged the woman from his tent. Sirocco leaned back on his pillows, glancing at the wound on his arm. He would not be weak before anyone again.

Sirocco tightened his grip on the clan as the days past. Aljilani had been well liked and his family extremely loyal. Two of his wives fled into the desert and had to be tracked down; one fought so hard his men were forced to kill her. The slaves were equally rebellious which was especially surprising. The iklan were usually fatalistic about such transitions for no matter who they answered to their status remained the same. Sirocco was forced to sell them. His mood darkened with each defiant event, his blame directed towards the witch and her failed talisman.

Three weeks later his men returned from the Sahel accompanied by a new sorceress. The woman rode on a camel draped with fine silks and ornaments, her face covered in the custom of the people inhabiting the Sahel. The richness of her camel and clothing turned the eyes of everyone, including Sirocco. She resembled a bride as she was led to his tent. Her camel kneeled without a gesture and she stepped gingerly into the sand. She sauntered up to the chieftain, her dark eyes intense and alluring.

"El Sirocco," she said. Her voice was sweet like dates. "I am Baramousso of Kano. Your men insisted that I visit you. It seems you are in need of a reliable sorceress."

Sirocco said nothing, mesmerized by the woman's enchanting grey eyes.

"El Sirocco?"

The repeat of his name broke his trance. "Yes, I am in need."

The woman closed her eyes and nodded. "I understand your former sorceress did not live up to your expectations."

The thought of the old woman focused his thoughts. "She was useless and now she is dead."

"I assure you I am far from useless, my chieftain. I possess many talents. Nyama is only one of them."

There was no doubt to the meaning of her words.

"Leave us," he ordered.

Sirocco and Baramousso stood alone regarding each other. The sorceress surprised him, removing her veil to reveal a face as lovely as her eyes. Her flawless ebony skin highlighted her mysterious eyes, her full lips inviting his attention as she smiled. She reached her hand into the bag hanging off her shoulders and extracted a talisman bag.

"I think this is what you need?" she said.

Sirocco reached out to take the bag from her and their hands touched. Heat flashed throughout his body, sparking desire beyond any he ever experienced. He draped the bag over his head and immediately felt the effect. This was powerful magic, much more intense than that of the old woman.

"You have skills," he said. He grasped her around the waist, pulling her to him. The sorceress didn't struggle.

"And what will you pay for this pleasure?" she whispered.

"I am The Desert Wind," he replied. "What I offer to you is a privilege."

"To some, but not to me," the sorceress replied. "I have found myself in this…position with men much more powerful than you. You may see yourself as great, but I see a bandit in the desert."

Sirocco's desire overwhelmed her insults. "Ask and it is yours."

The sorceress smiled. "Make me your first wife and I will make you a king. You feel my power now. It will be tenfold when we consummate this union. No one will be able to stand before you. You will have no one to fear."

Sirocco pushed down his shesh and kissed her hard, reveling in the taste of the lips that had taunted him since she entered his tent. Their tongues laced together like amorous vines, her breath thick and sweet like honey.

"You are my wife," he said. "You are my queen."

Baramousso removed his shesh completely. "You are mine now, Sirocco."

They removed each other's clothes and tumbled onto the pillows.

* * *

It was dark when he awoke. The voices around him were urgent and fearful. Sirocco attempted to rise but his arms and legs would not move. Something wet touched his face; his bodyguards lay on the ground near him, blood pouring from the slits across their throats. Again, he tried to rise but could not. He felt as if a stone had been set upon him.

"He's awake!" a male voice exclaimed.

"It doesn't matter," the sorceress replied. "The potion paralyzed him. You have nothing to fear."

Hands grabbed his clothes and rolled him onto his back. Baramousso stared down on him, contempt in her eyes. She spat in his face.

"Tuareg dog!" she hissed. "Did you really believe you were important enough to possess me? I can't wait to return to Djenne to wash off your stink."

She kicked him hard in the ribcage. "You should be careful who you kill. Akuji was well respected among us. True, her skills had diminished, but she deserved your respect. She saw promise in you, but she was wrong."

A man appeared beside her. Sirocco recognized him immediately; he was a Songhai cavalryman.

"The Askia will pay a handsome ransom for this one," he commented.

"This has nothing to do with gold," the sorceress said. "He belongs to me. Your king receives the loot from the kel and I get him. That was our agreement."

The cavalryman looked disappointed. "It is as you say."

Sirocco listened to the discussion on his fate with a mixture of anger and despair. If he had his swords they both would be dead; if he had kept his wits he would be standing before them. The sorceress looked at him as if she could hear his thoughts.

"Take him to my camels," she ordered.

Two cavalrymen lifted him and carried him out of his tent and into the night. Bodies lay strewn among burning tents, thick black smoke rising into the night sky obscuring the stars. Songhai *sofas* looted his possessions, using the camels that once belong to him. The men draped him across a camel and tied him to the beast. After checking the ropes, they look at his face and laughed.

"Too bad you're not going with us," one of them said. "Your death would be swift. You'll probably end up in someone's talisman bag."

The men laughed again and walked away. Minutes later the sorceress appeared, shoving something bitter into his mouth. His eyes became heavy; he struggled to see but the substance dragged him into an empty darkness. As he slid into oblivion he heard sorceress's voice.

"Death is too good for you, El Sirocco. I have something much better in mind."

* * *

Damp air touched El Sirocco's skin and he flinched. He opened his eyes and winched at the bright sun looming overhead. Shapes came into view, rugged mountains awash with green vegetation and crowned with whiteness. A sound like the rushing wind opened his ears, constant and unending. The smell that burned his nose was unknown to him as well. The weight that held him down was gone and his hands were free. He sat up and heard a loud crack followed by a burning sting creasing across his back.

"Good, you can walk now," a husky voice shouted. A boot met his ribs and he fell onto hard dark earth. He looked up into the rigid face of a bearded man with eyes as cold as a desert night. It was then that he realized his shesh was gone. His hands went to his face, attempting to protect his mouth from the evil spewing from the bearded man's gaze.

"What's wrong with him?" the man asked. "Did the woman sell us a crazy Tuareg?"

A robed man came shuffling up to him, his hands holding a length of soiled fabric. Sirocco recognized the type; he was Bedouin. He was also a slave.

"His face needs to be covered," the Bedouin explained. "It is the way of his people." The Bedouin halted a safe distance away, extending the cloth to Sirocco.

"I know your people prefer blue, but it is all I have," the man whispered.

Sirocco took the cloth, wrapping it around his face and head. It stank, but the smell was worth the protection. He stood and looked about. He was not a part of a slave caravan; there was only him, the Bedouin and the evil man. The land was like nothing he'd ever seen, rich with water and greener that the most abundant oasis. To his people this would resemble paradise but he suspected something much less pleasant. He sized up the man who apparently was his master and grinned under his homemade shesh.

"Try it, I dare you!" the man shouted. "The woman told me you would. She gave me something special in case you did."

The man removed a talisman bag from under his soiled shirt. "If I die, you die."

Sirocco did not doubt him. Baramousso had more that demonstrated her power. She had promised him power and taken it away, sentencing him to a life that to an Ihaggaren was worse than death.

"Don't worry, you'll get your chance," the man said. "You Tuaregs are useless when it comes to labor, but you're damn good fighters. You'll make me rich in Mogadishu."

Sirocco said nothing. He looked away from the man, focusing his eyes on the clouds drifting among the mountaintops. He had no idea where he was; his power had been stripped from him, his people slaughtered. It was a fair punishment. He had put his faith in the wrong hands and paid for it.

"Praise to Allah we are still alive, brother," the Bedouin said. His words stirred something inside Sirocco, memories of a faith long dead inside of him, a path he had abandoned long ago. Allah was punishing him for his sins, banishing him to this unknown land and condemning him to the life of a slave. A lesser man would fall to his knees and beg forgiveness, groveling for The Prophet's mercy. But Sirocco was no such man. He decided he would accept this challenge, following it wherever it would lead. If it led one day back to his home he would have his revenge. If not, then that was his fate.

"Faster, you piles of camel shit!" the man exclaimed. "I don't want to be on this road after dark!"

Sirocco fell into step with the oxen. His old life was done. His new life, whatever it would be, lay ahead. He had triumphed before; he would triumph again.

"Let's go, Tuareg," the man shouted.

The man once known as Sirocco grinned and obeyed.

MREMBO ALIYENASWA
(CAPTURED BEAUTY)

Spectators crowded the bulwark of the Sada, filling the merchant dhow from stern to bow. Those that couldn't find room on the deck hung from mast ropes and sat on the bulwark. Their eyes focused on two bare-chested men circling each other, their brown skin glistening with sweat. The taller man lumbered from side to side, his huge arms swaying as he tried to keep pace with his shorter opponent. He possessed a wide chest and a wider stomach sitting on legs that resembled thick tree trunks. His short-curled hair atop his head contrasted with the voluminous beard grazing his chest with each frustrating turn of his head.

The other man moved with martial grace, his body a chiseled muscular form. His smooth face and bald head told of his youth, but his deep brown eyes revealed experience beyond his years. He observed his opponent with the skill of a man used to such encounters, a man whose battles in his past usually ended in death. Luckily for the big man, this was not such an encounter.

"Stand still, Changa!" the big man bellowed. "How do you expect me to give you a hug if you keep flittering like a moth?"

The spectators laughed and Changa grinned. "I'm no fool, Yusef. Those arms were meant to hug tembos, not men, and certainly not women."

Yusef lunged at Changa. Changa dodged to his left, slapping Yusef across the forehead with an open right hand. The big man stopped just short of plowing into the crowd of terrified baharia.

"Damn you, kibwana!" Yusef yelled. "Stand still! From Mogadishu to Mombasa they call you Mbogo, The Bull. All I see is a skittish little fish."

Changa laughed at the insult. He planted his feet, resting his hands at his waist.

"Come then. Let's see if your clumsy hands can crush this little fish."

The two inched towards each other, their arms extended. Their fingers touched then intertwined as they began a test of strength as old as time.

"Hah!" Yusef shouted. He pressed down on Changa, tightening his massive hands around Changa's. A normal man would have crumbled under the huge man's weight; a strong man would have buckled in seconds. Changa stood still, the only indication of exertion the rippling muscles under his taunt black skin. Yusef pressed harder and Changa remained unmoved. The giant lost his humor; he clenched his teeth and pressed harder, his arms shaking with effort. Changa did not budge. Every man on the dhow fell silent to the amazing test of strength playing out before them. None doubted Changa's strength, but this display went far beyond their imagining.

While Yusef and the others interpreted Changa's silence as an unbelievable show of poise, the opposite was true. Changa concentrated with every pound of his muscle, fighting back Yusef's onslaught. He was lapping at the brink of his endurance, waiting the right moment. He looked into his opponent's frustrated face and determined the time was right.

Changa collapsed. A triumphant grin emerged through Yusef's beard until he realized Changa wasn't falling; he was rolling. He was too committed to pull back. Pain shot from his belly to his back as Changa drove his feet into Yusef's belly. The big man was airborne, Changa's face replaced by sails, seagulls and sky. His brief flight ended amidst a crowd of hands, feet, bodies and groans as he landed among the unfortunate baharia on the deck.

"Mbogo!" the uninjured spectators cheered. Changa rolled to his feet then sauntered to Yusef and the pile of hapless victims beneath him.

"You were right," Changa said as he massaged his sore arms and shoulders "You are stronger than me."

"Are you done playing, Changa?" Kasim, the dhow captain walked between the two. The Sada sailors scurried to their chores at the sight of their captain, the others dispersing to their duties at the docks.

Changa looked down at Yusef, extending his hand. "Are we done?"

Yusef took Changa's hand and Changa pulled him up to a sitting position.

"Yes, we are done…Mbogo," he conceded, a defeated tone in his voice.

Kasim nodded. "Good. Belay wants to see you right away."

Changa's mood shifted from victorious to serious. He hurried below and washed himself, donned his cotton shirt and proceeded to the warehouse containing Belay's office. The merchant sat hunched over his desk as always, studying his counting books.

"Bwana, you sent for me?" Changa asked.

Belay looked up, greeting Changa with a broad grin.

"Yes, Changa. Please, sit down."

Belay leaned back in his chair and massaged his forehead.

"I don't understand why Allah punishes me. I pray, I am a fair and honest man and I give alms to the poor. Instead of blessing me he brings me troubles."

"It is never more than you can handle," Changa said.

"So you say," Belay sighed. "Do you know Mustafa the goat herder?"

"Barely."

"I'm sure you know of his daughter, Yasmine."

Changa answered with a smile. In a city known for its beautiful women Yasmine stood out like a diamond among broken stones. Not a single man in Mombasa, Changa included, would hesitate to accumulate a generous lobola if he knew she favored him.

Changa's scowl answered Belay's question. "Mustafa barges in my office this morning demanding to see me. Being the Muslim that I am, I allowed him an audience despite his rudeness. He sat where you sit now and stated that Yasmine was missing and Naragisi was to blame."

Changa's face and he shifted in his seat. Naragisi was Belay's eldest son, as different from his father as oil and water. He was a vain and selfish man with the spirit of Shaitan.

"I know what you're thinking," Belay said. "You think Mustafa is right. I think so, too, but I could not say so in front of him. I told him I would look into the matter and you know what he did? He jumped to his feet and slammed his fist on my desk! He demanded that I either return his daughter or pay him twice the lobola offered by her suitors."

"I have seen Naragisi courting Yasmine," Changa said. "She did not seem pleased with his attention."

Belay stood. "We will visit him immediately and get to the root of this."

Changa stood as well. "If we go to see Naragisi we'll need men."

Belay rubbed his forehead again. "Yes, that's true. Will you see to it, Changa?"

"Of course, bwana."

Changa returned to the dhow burdened with concern. Men gathered about him as soon as he boarded.

"Bashiri, Zakwani and Tayari, get your weapons," he announced. "We're escorting Bwana Belay to Naragisi's house."

The chosen men hurried below deck with huge grins on their faces. Escort duty was extra pay. Going with Changa meant they had a good chance of returning. Changa noticed Yusef sulking across the ship, still smarting from his recent defeat.

"Yusef," he called out. "Get your gear. You're coming, too."

The big man smiled like a child. "Of course, Changa, of course!"

The men met Belay at the warehouse. Belay climbed on his wagon and they set out for the mainland. After a brief stop in the country town to gather supplies they set out for the bush. Naragisi's difference from his father went beyond personalities. Unlike most Swahili Naragisi despised the stone town, preferring life in the hinterlands. They reached his estate by daybreak the next day, the impressive two-story house rising over the otherwise flat landscape. An expansive shamba filled with hundreds of Zebu cattle surrounded his elaborate home, the estate protected by Samburu warriors. Instead of the normal thorn bush palisade Naragisi had constructed a stone wall six feet high. Four stone gates allowed entrance, one at each point of the compass, each protected by a Samburu village. Changa and the others met no opposition until they reached the gate. Four Samburu guarded the gate, tall lean men with iron tipped spears and swords that flared out like fans at the tip. A red cloak fell from one shoulder, covering their bodies to the knees. A black beaded belt gathered the cloak about their waists and held the wooden scabbards for their swords and daggers. Each warrior held a broad leaf shield of cowhide, the pattern of Naragisi painted on each one.

The guards shifted as Changa approached them.

"Habare," Changa said.

"Umzuri," the guards replied.

"Bwana Belay wishes to see his son."

"That is not possible," the warrior replied. "Bwana Naragisi is not to be disturbed."

Suspicion emerged in Changa's thoughts, confirmed by the look in Belay's eyes.

"Must I remind you where your master's wealth originates?" Belay said.

The Samburu guards shifted their stances. "Our master's wealth resides within his walls," the warrior sneered. "Golden metal has no value here."

Changa's snatched his sword from its sheath before the guards could react, its tip pressed into the warrior's chin.

"Is your master's wealth worth your life?"

The warrior opened the gate and stepped aside. The Mombassans crossed the wide expanse to the door of Naragisi's home. A servant girl dressed in a colorful kanga and beaded braids met them at the entrance.

"Welcome, baba," she said respectfully. "Your son is grateful you have come to visit him. Please follow me to the veranda."

The girl led them to a huge courtyard, the stone floor covered by an enormous and expensive Persian rug. An elaborate table was set before them. Belay sat at the table; Changa, Yusef and the others remained standing behind him.

Naragisi entered accompanied by a dozen Samburu warriors. He dressed simply, white pants and long shirt with a caramel vest. A small turban hugged his head held together by an amber broach. He smiled at his father as he cut a glance at Changa.

"Baba, welcome!" he said. "I am so glad you came to visit me so unexpectedly."

"I have no time for your deception, Naragisi," Belay retorted. "Mustafa the goat herder came to my warehouse today, claiming you had something to do with Yasmine's disappearance. Do you?"

Naragisi sat at the table, taking time to prepare a cup of chai.

"He is Yasmine's father, is he not?"

Belay's small hands clenched. "Yes, he is."

"Hmm." Naragisi sipped his tea. "Yes and no."

"What do you mean yes and no?"

"Yes, father, I am responsible for Yasmine's disappearance, but not in the way you suspect."

Changa's hand went to his sword and Naragisi's guards responded by stepping forward, their spears lowered.

Belay raised his hand. "I didn't come here for violence. I came here for answers."

"It's no secret I wanted Yasmine," Naragisi admitted. "I waited for her to arrive at the market every day and gave her gifts and kind words. It was more than any woman of her station deserved no matter how beautiful she is. She should have been grateful."

Naragisi paused to sip his tea again. A frown marred his face.

"I finally explained to her my intentions and she laughed. She laughed at me! I wanted to strike her down and I would have if I didn't cherish her beauty so much. I decided to show her what being my wife meant. I arranged to have her brought here."

"You had her kidnapped," Changa said.

"No one gave you permission to speak, mtwana," Naragisi growled.

"Keep your insults!" Belay barked. "Who did you hire?"

Naragisi leaned back on his cushion and raised his teacup, staring at Changa.

"Wal Wasaki."

Belay sighed, closed his eyes and hung his head. Changa fought a surge of anger as he struggled to keep his hand from his sword.

"I thought Wal would bring her to me," Naragisi continued. "We have conducted business before."

"Wasaki deals with the highest bidder," Changa said. "He must have received a better offer."

"You keep speaking as if it matters," Naragisi commented.

Changa was about to answer when Belay raised his hand.

"Enough!" Belay stood. "I'll deal with you latter, Naragisi."

Belay exited the room and the others followed. Changa hesitated; watching Naragisi and his men to make sure Belay's departure was safe. He turned to leave.

"Changa," Naragisi called out.

Changa turned slowly and was met by Naragisi's cold eyes.

"My father is a *mwungwana*. He's well respected for his intelligence, generosity and piety. Your status in Mombasa depends on him."

"I know this," Changa snapped. "You're wasting your words and my time."

Naragisi's eyes narrowed. "My father will not live forever."

Changa smirked. "Neither will you."

He backed out the room and trotted to catch up with his party.

Changa watched Belay with disappointment as they returned to Mombasa. Belay would do nothing to Naragisi. His sons were worthless but the old merchant loved them too much to punish them. He would ignore his son's crime and attempt to ease Mustafa's suffering with payment and favors. When they reached Belay's home at nightfall Changa was the first to speak.

"Bwana, let me deal with Wal," he said.

"That won't be necessary, Changa. Wal is a criminal, but he is also a businessman. I'll pay him whatever he asks."

"What if he doesn't have her?"

Belay sighed. "Then there is nothing more I can do."

"I will deliver your offer," Changa said. "If he does not have Yasmine I will find out where she is."

"And how will you accomplish this?" Belay inquired.

"I can be very persuasive," Changa smiled.

Belay returned his smile. "Take good men with you, Changa. Don't do anything…foolish."

"I will be careful, bwana."

* * *

Wal Wasaki's compound was only a few miles from Belay's warehouse in the center of Low Town. Though the distance between the two sections was brief, the contrast was jarring. Entering Low Town was like walking into a tempest. The thick grey walls surrounding the district were remnants from a time when Low Town served as Mombasa's prison. A strange order existed within the barricades, a chaotic system that changed with the whims of its master, Wal Wasaki, a man who was as brilliant as he was mad. Changa thought on this as he and his cohorts approached the western gate.

"This is the nearest entrance to Wal's main compound," he told the others. "We must be swift if we expect to confront him."

"I thought we were supposed to offer him payment," Yusef said.

Changa grinned at the big man. "We will, but we'll add a little incentive." He patted his knife bag.

Yusef grinned back. "I like you, kibwana."

Changa and his cohorts entered Wal's realm purposely, their countenances revealing their intent. It was obvious they were looking for someone. The reaction of the onlookers varied; some ran, some fell to their knees in prayer while others slipped silently into the refuge of nearby buildings. Then there were those that stood defiantly, their hands gripping daggers or swords, ready to face the danger the armed interlopers presented.

Wal's compound occupied the center of his district. Thick stone walls topped by jagged metal spikes encased the elaborate buildings inside. Two heavily armed guards flanked the iron gate, watching Changa and his men with little concern. Changa continued past them as he eased his hand into his knife bag, waiting until Yusef was before them. He turned, throwing his knife at the guard closest to him. The knife struck the man in the head and he crumpled where he stood. The second guard threw up his shield, deflecting Changa's second knife. Yusef pounced, knocking away the shield with his left fist as he drove his sword into the man's gut. Changa sprinted by the dying man, leading the attack into Wal's compound.

Changa kicked the gate open and charged into the compound. He ran directly to the largest home surrounded by more guards. They looked stunned until they realized

Changa's intent. Changa's companions surged around him and attacked the guards. Changa hurried through the fray, looking for Wal. He spotted the bandit slipping out the rear of his home, accompanied by two guards. He pursued them, a throwing knife in each hand. He drew his arm back and threw both knives, striking both guards in the back. Wal spun about, his sword drawn.

"This is a foolish thing you do, Changa," he said.

Changa ignored Wal's threat. He dodged the bandit's weak thrust and punched him across the jaw, knocking him senseless. He grabbed the bandit by the collar of his shirt and dragged him into the house.

Yusef and the others met him inside. The house was a miniature palace, decorated with items from throughout Swahililand and the world. A huge Persian rug covered the entire tile floor. Aromatic incenses burned in lamps in every corner. Large silk pillows rested at the center of the rug, surrounding a group of women clutching each other and whimpering. Bowls of food were overturned, a sign of Wal's hasty exit.

Changa's men rushed the women from the room while he towed Wal to the center. He shoved the man to the floor and dropped his foot on his chest, his sword tip to his throat.

"Wal Wasaki, I come on behalf of Belay. He wishes to know the whereabouts of Yasmine, daughter of Mustafa. He has authorized me to pay for this information."

"You're a fool, Changa, a fool!" Wal spat.

Changa stepped away from Wal and signaled Yusef. The big Swahili snatched Wal from the rug, raised the man over his head and threw him across the room. Wal slammed into the wall and crashed to the floor.

"Yusef!" Changa yelled.

The big man held out his hands and shrugged. Changa glared at him as he ran to Wal. The bandit was still alive.

"Where is Yasmine?" he asked.

Wal stirred. "Sheik Abdul," he whispered.

Changa bent closer, refusing to acknowledge what he heard. "What did you say?"

Wal winced as he rolled onto his back. "I sold her to Sheik Abdul of Zanzibar."

Changa closed his eyes, a curse slipping from his lips. It was worse than he imagined.

"She is lost then," he said.

Wal managed to laugh. "Do you think Abdul would come to me for a common slave? He could get that from any of a hundred slavers working the coast. Yasmine was special. Her life with Abdul will be better that she deserves, much better than living with Naragisi surrounded by savages and cow shit."

Changa wanted to drive his sword between Wal's shoulders but he didn't come to kill the man. He dropped the bag of gold by Wal's face.

"Your payment." Changa stepped away, signaling Yusef and the others. They emerged into an eerie silence, their exit much quieter than their entrance. Yusef found his way to Changa's side.

"That was good, kibwana. Belay will be happy."

Changa nodded.

Yusef scratched his beard. "I don't understand why you paid him."

"The payment will allow Wal to save face," Changa answered. "It will also keep us alive. Wal wouldn't allow us to live if word spread of what we did. He wouldn't touch Belay for that would risk vendetta. But we're nothing to him. He'd keep sending assassins until we were all dead."

Changa and his companions relaxed once they emerged from Wal's district. They headed directly to Belay's warehouse with their news.

Belay paced as he spoke. "Wal may be right about Yasmine's fate."

Changa was confused. "You agree with him, bwana?"

"Yasmine may be better off with Abdul," Belay reasoned. "Her virtue has been compromised. No man will marry her now, not even Naragisi. She will have a good life as Abdul's concubine."

Changa bristled. "She will still be a slave. She has no one to protect her from the whims of Abdul. What if he tires of her? She'll be cast into the masses. Yasmine should not be punished for her beauty. She did not ask for this fate."

Belay stopped pacing and looked at Changa with sympathy. "Your feelings are personal and you raise valid questions. However, I did not make the world."

"She should have a choice," Changa retorted. He was pushing his authority, spurred by shame of his memories. "This was Naragisi's doing. You are always correcting his mistakes. You should correct this."

Belay dropped his head. "That is true. I would be a much richer man if not for the debts of my sons. Prepare the Sada. We will sail to Zanzibar and meet with Sheik Abdul. We will see how much a concubine is worth these days."

*   *   *

The Sada sailed into the harbor of Zanzibar on a clear, cloudless day. Belay sent messengers to Abdul as soon as they docked. The Mombassans awaited the sheik's reply on board. Changa did not take part in the dhows chores; he, Yusef and others were present as Belay's bodyguards. The messengers returned quickly. Sheik Abdul would meet with them in three days.

While Belay took the time to conduct business, Changa's anxiousness grew. His mind kept slipping back to his early days of captivity. He followed Belay about in angry silence, the minutes passing like eternity. When the day finally came for the meeting, Changa's mood was at the least tense.

Sheik Abdul's palace lay south of the harbor, surrounded by the slave pens. Changa tried to ignore the human cages but his eyes betrayed him. Hundreds of people lay chained in the filthy compartments waiting to be sold to slavers who would take them north to Arabia and beyond. He looked into their desperate eyes and saw a sense of hopelessness far beyond anything he ever experienced while similarly confined. Abdul's control was more than physical; there was something deeper at work.

One pair of eyes caught his attention. They belonged to a boy clutching the bars with emaciated fingers. Changa found himself falling into the boy's gaze until he looked into the streets of Zanzibar from the cage. He saw dense forest as the cage rocked back and forth with the contours of the wooded hills as the caravan travelled the muddy road leading from his city, his kingdom and his family. The fear of an eight-year-old boy returned, the terror of a child that saw his father murdered and his mothers and sisters taken as wives of the murderer.

"Kibwana, are you well?"

Yusef's deep intrusive voice shattered his waking nightmare.

"I'm fine."

They stood before Abdul's palace. A servant greeted them at the gates, a welcoming smile on his face.

"Welcome, Bwana Belay. My master awaits you in the veranda."

The servant led them through the gates to the veranda. Sheik Abdul sat before a table filled with food and sweets, a banquet fit for a dignitary. A solemn servant offered Belay a seat. Changa and Yusef flanked the merchant.

Abdul nodded to Belay. "Welcome, my brother. This is a pleasant surprise. I have heard much of you and I am flattered by your visit."

Belay nodded in return. "The reputation of Abdul sails on the sea as far as the Spice Lands. I am flattered you granted my request."

Abdul nodded to a servant who poured him a glass of wine. Changa noticed the same look in the woman's eyes like the boy in the cage, a vacuous vision of despair.

"I can't believe we've never met before," Abdul continued. "Belay of Mombasa is a man well known throughout Swahililand."

Belay refrained from wine, preferring water. "Sheik Abdul is a legend among merchants."

Abdul closed his eyes as he replied. "I am but a humble man. But tell me, rafiki; is it business that finds you here this day?"

"Yes, but not the type you are familiar with."

Abdul's face looked puzzled. "Surely a man with wealth such as yours has need of what I provide?"

"I own no plantations," Belay replied. "I prefer the exchange of goods to the fruits of the earth."

Abdul took an orange from his bowl. "Slaves can be docile as cows if properly trained. I seem to recall there is one in your employ that may be an exception."

Abdul's eyes rested on Changa. Belay glanced at the Bakongo and smiled.

"I freed Changa soon after rescuing him from the fighting pit. A man with his skills and abilities didn't deserve to be a slave."

"No one does," Abdul agreed. "But we did not make the world."

"That is true."

The two carried on a casual conversation as they ate. Changa glared at Abdul, his distaste for the man growing with every minute past. There was something missing in a man like Abdul, an emptiness of that allowed them to treat some men like objects while showing kindness to others.

The servants cleared the table. Belay leaned back in his chair, rubbing his stomach.

"An excellent feast," he said.

"I'm humbled by your praise." Abdul took another cup of wine. "Now my friend, why have you come?"

"I'm here to make right a wrong committed by my son. I was told you purchased a woman from Wal Wasaki, a woman my son had kidnapped for refusing his marriage offer. I have come to buy her back."

Abdul's face contorted in confusion. "I do not know of what you speak. I do conduct business with Wasaki occasionally, but I never deal directly with him. Maybe one of my men has seen this woman. Can you describe her?"

"She needs no description, for she is a queen among queens. Her beauty knows no rival and her virtue honors her family. That is why it is so important that I do this. The woman is innocent."

Abdul rubbed his chin. "I would remember such a woman. What is her name?"

"Yasmine."

Abdul folded his jeweled hands in his lap; a lie glimmered in his eyes before escaping his lips.

"I'm sorry, my friend. I have not seen this Yasmine. A woman such as you described would be very valuable, not for what she possesses in beauty but for what she may harbor within. If I did come across such a woman, I would not be able to part with her. She would be priceless."

Changa coughed to keep from cursing. Abdul's eyes narrowed as they took in the Bakongo, the threat emanating from them clear. Belay saw the exchange and stood.

"I will not waste anymore of your time, Abdul. I realized this might be a fruitless journey but I had to try. I thank you for your time and hospitality."

Abdul came to Belay and they hugged. "You must come again soon," Abdul said. "The hunting on the southern tip of the island is excellent."

"I will," Belay replied. "Allah be with you."

"And with you."

Changa's restraint failed him as soon as he set foot on the Sada.

"He has her!"

Belay sat at his desk in the cabin. "I know."

"You should have made him an offer."

Belay sighed. "He would have refused. Yasmine's beauty seems to be a curse to her."

Changa slammed his fist as against the wall. "You didn't even try!"

Belay came to his feet. "Enough, Changa! If you hope to be a merchant one day you must learn keep your personal feelings under control. This is business."

"No, bwana, it is not. This is about a person's life."

"This became business the moment Wal took Yasmine. I have done all I can do. We are finished with this matter, you hear me? When we return to Mombasa I will pay Mustafa a proper lobola."

Changa's glare subsided into a disappointed stare.

"Go see about the crew," Belay commanded. "We leave in the morning."

Night had descended on Zanzibar when Changa finished his inspection. He went immediately to his cabin, gathered his weapons and returned to the deck.

"Where are you going, kibwana?"

Yusef leaned against the main mast, his thick arms folded across his chest.

"Go back below," Changa advised. "This doesn't concern you."

"You're going to get Yasmine, aren't you?"

Changa ignored the big man as he walked down the plank. Yusef strode toward him.

"I'm going with you."

Changa turned, looking up into Yusef's defiant eyes.

"Don't be ridiculous."

"You defeated me in front of everyone," Yusef answered. "If I wish a chance to redeem myself I need to make sure you come back alive."

"I won't slow down for you," Changa warned.

"You won't have to," Yusef smiled.

The two made their way to the dark streets of Zanzibar. Changa set a fast pace and Yusef, true to his word, kept pace. They reached Abdul's palace in moments, the streets strangely quiet for such a large town.

Changa went immediately to the compound. He leapt onto the wall like a panther then jumped down into the courtyard, sword drawn. The courtyard was unguarded, unusual for a compound that held such wealth. He went to the gate and let Yusef in. They crept to the palace door. Changa tested it and it held firm.

"Stand aside, kibwana," Yusef whispered.

"This is not the time for brute strength," Changa warned.

"You insult me," Yusef replied.

The big Mombassan leaned against the door until he heard a cracking sound. Yusef stepped away and pushed the door open effortlessly.

The faint scuff of padded paws was the only warning. Changa instinctively jumped aside and the black leopard flashed by him, slamming into Yusef's chest. He moved to help his friend but suddenly found himself dodging the charge of another leopard. The beast opened its mouth in a silent roar as it crept towards him. Changa backed away, brandishing a throwing knife in each hand. The cat struck out with its paw and Changa struck back, batting the claws away. The silence was shattered by Yusef's bellow and the leopard's cohort sailed out the doorway, landing lifeless in the dirt. Changa's attacker was distracted for a moment, which was all the time he needed. A knife flew from his hand into the leopard's breast and the cat rose up on its hind legs, grasping the knife with its forelimbs. Changa's second knife ripped into the feline's belly and it fell onto its back. He finished it with his sword, driving the point into the leopard's throat.

He ran inside and found Yusef slumped against the wall, bleeding from his shoulder and chest.

"We have to go back," Changa said. "You need help."

"No!" Yusef snapped. "These are scratches, nothing more. We came for Yasmine."

Yusef stood unsteadily. "Lead the way, kibwana, unless those kittens stole your nerve."

Changa smirked as he re-entered the house. The foyer was pitch black so he felt along the wall, searching for a torch when he heard the twang of bowstrings. He dropped quickly and rolled to his left, pulling out his throwing knives as he came to his feet. The strings thumped again and he heard Yusef grunt. Changa threw his knife at the bow sound and was rewarded with a painful cry. He moved again and the arrow meant for his throat clattered against the stone wall. Changa threw a second knife. It missed its mark but accomplished its goal. The archer opened a door across the room to escape, a stream of torchlight seeping into the room. Changa ran back to check on Yusef and found him sitting at the entrance, an arrow protruding from his shoulder. The big man grasped the arrow and broke it.

"A pin prick," he said.

"Stay here," Changa ordered. He chased after the bowman, entering a corridor lit by a succession of torches. The sound of footfalls from behind alarmed him and he spun about, his sword and knife on guard. Yusef was on his feet, wincing as he lumbered through the open door.

"Go back," Changa urged.

"No, kibwana, I'm staying with you."

They crept down the hall in pursuit of the bowman. Changa's instincts were on edge; the house felt wrong. Abdul was a rich man; his house should have been filled with people and possessions. With the exception of the bowman they had encountered no one.

A door at the end of the hall was opened slightly. Changa saw a smattering of blood staining the white marble floor. Something more escaped from the room, something sensed rather than seen. Changa reached for the door and stopped.

Yusef eased up behind him. "What are we waiting for?"

"Can't you feel it?" Changa whispered.

Yusef shook his head. "Feel what?"

Changa turned to his companion. "Something is not right."

The big man was around Changa and through the door before Changa could stop him. He hesitated, listening for some response to Yusef's intrusion but there was none. His curiosity overcame his stealth and he entered the room.

Yusef stood frozen. The bowman lay dead a few feet before the Mombassan. Beyond them both in the center of the room was a large dais. Sitting on the surface was Yasmine. She was naked, her arms and legs chained to thick iron loops protruding from the stone. A blank expression ruled her face as she stared at Changa. He felt her spirit reaching into his mind like loving fingers; his arms fell limp to his sides and he dropped his weapons. The clattering metal pulled him from Yasmine's hypnotic gaze. He heard Yusef grunt and jerked his head about to see Yusef raising his sword at him.

"Yusef, no!" Changa shouted. Yusef raised his scimitar high then slashed down. Changa dodged the swipe then ducked the swing aimed at his neck. Yusef moved faster than Changa thought capable of a man of his size. Changa danced away knowing he had no chance stopping those powerful blows. Yasmine controlled him, driving him far beyond his abilities. Changa could not stop Yusef but he could stop Yasmine.

He dodged another swing, jumping between Yusef and the dais. He snatched out a throwing knife, holding it by the blade. The edge sliced his hand and he threw it at Yasmine, the handle striking her on the head and sprawling her on the dais. Yusef fell as she fell, crashing onto the floor in a massive heap.

Changa ran to his unconscious companion. Yusef panted, his body burning. Changa heard more footsteps. Dozens of armed men clad in chain mail and leather marched into the chamber, their eyes weighed with the same despondency Changa viewed among Abdul's slaves. They formed an armed barrier between the Mombassan and the dais. Abdul sauntered into the room and climbed onto the dais. He knelt beside Yasmine, cradling her injured head in his hands.

"You discovered my secret," he said as he smiled. "Do you know the power of beauty, Mombassan? Most men just see the surface, lusting for physical contact to satiate their shallow desires. But the power lies within. It is the power to manipulate and control. It's the reason why men fear women, why we spend so much time attempting to control that which we have no control."

Abdul propped Yasmine up, holding her face in his hands.

"But the true power lies deeper still. It is beyond women, a strength so deep it can only be tapped by ancient spells created at the beginning of time."

Abdul closed his eyes, whispering into Yasmine's ear. Her eyes snapped open and she sat erect. She leveled her blank white orbs on Changa and pain exploded behind his eyes. He dropped his weapons, clutching his head as the pain bored into his sanity. He was losing consciousness, blood running from his ears and nose. But then the pain went too far, touching a place within the Mombassan that even he never knew existed. Changa reared back and emitted a cry that startled Abdul

"No one controls me!" Changa yelled.

"Kill him!" Abdul yelled back.

Changa grabbed his throwing knife and hurled it at Abdul. The knife sunk into the slave master's head, knocking him from the dais to the floor. A wail rose from the compound, a collective cry of a thousand souls suddenly released from an evil stupor. The guards ran from the room, their faces bright with the prospect of freedom. Changa staggered to Abdul's body. He searched the man's robes and found a key ring. He was so weak the climb up the dais was like scaling a mountain. It took him a long moment to find the key for Yasmine's shackles. He freed the woman, and then lay at her side.

The urgent sounds of destruction awoke him. Men and women screamed, shouted and cursed in the distance. Swords rang out down the corridors and the smell of smoke hung heavy in the air. Changa rose to the hulking image of Yusef towering above him, his scimitar in his hand. He turned and looked down on Changa.

"So, kibwana, are you done with your nap?"

Changa struggle to his feet and Yasmine stirred. A painful moan escaped her lips.

"What's going on?" Changa asked.

"Chaos," Yusef replied. "Abdul's slaves are running rampant. The city guard is attempting to keep them in the compound."

Changa found his weapons. "Give me your scimitar," he said to Yusef. "Pick up Yasmine."

Changa took the sword and Yusef lifted Yasmine to his shoulders. Together they plunged into the chaos of the compound, pushing through desperate people and eventually found their way to the gates. Guardsmen blocked the way, their pikes lowered as they secured the gates from the outside. Changa sheathed his sword and stepped a few paces from the wall. He ran and jumped, his fingertips landing on the wall's edge. With a loud grunt he lifted himself onto the wall then jumped down into the midst of the guards. Changa's sword was out and slashing before the soldiers knew what happening. In moments he stood surrounded by dying men.

"Pull down the gate!" he shouted. The men inside grasped the bars, jerking with all their strength. Changa turned his back to them as more guardsmen appeared. He never considered the overwhelming odds; he gripped his sword and waiting for their assault. The gate gave way just as the guardsmen reached Changa. A human flood surged past him, overwhelming the hapless guards. Changa found Yasmine and Yusef and they ran towards the docks. The streets swarmed with people, some fleeing for their freedom, some fleeing for their lives while the city guard fought to restore order. Changa and the others reached the dock as Belay's baharia hastily untied the Sara. The sailors crowded around their friends and Yasmine as they carried her aboard.

Yusef knocked them away. "Have some decency!" he bellowed. He removed his shirt, wrapping it around the woman. Yasmine looked up at her saviors and smiled.

"Thank you," she whispered.

"Make way! Make way!"

The baharia parted for Belay. He looked at the woman, Changa and Yusef.

"So, you're the cause of this," he said.

"Yes, bwana," Changa replied.

"You disobeyed me."

Changa looked at Belay defiantly. "I did what was right."

A relieved smile came to the merchant's face. "I'm glad you did."

He knelt beside Yasmine. "We will take you home, daughter. Your family will be happy to see you."

Belay stood and the stern expression returned to his face. "What are you dogs looking at? Get us out of here. I'm losing money with all you standing around!"

The sails unfurled and the dhow fled the harbor of Zanzibar. Changa led Yasmine below deck and into his cabin.

"You will be safe now," he said. "I give you my word."

Yasmine touched his face and kissed his cheek. "You are a brave man. If by chance you decide to offer lobola to my father it would be a happy day for me."

She entered the cabin and smiled again before Changa closed the door.

Changa turned to the sound of approaching footsteps. Belay walked up to him and hugged him.

"You are the son I should have had," he announced. "You may not be of my blood, but you have my spirit. When we return to Mombasa I will proclaim it so."

"That is not necessary," Changa replied. "You are already a father to me."

Belay beamed as he walked away. Changa was proud of Belay's promise, but he was most proud of rescuing Yasmine. He hoped that one day he could do the same for those he left behind so long ago.

"Are you done?"

Yusef loomed above him, his wounds patched by the ship's healer. A grin creased Changa's face.

"Yes, I am," he replied.

Yusef smiled back. "Good. We have unfinished business in Mombasa, Mbogo."

Changa swatted the big man on his wounded shoulder and he winched.

"You'll get your chance."

Yusef swatted him back. "Don't run away from me this time, kibwana."

Changa rubbed his aching shoulder and smiled.

"Don't worry," he said. "This time I won't have to."

THE SEA PRIEST

Mikaili opened his senses to the sights and smell of the sea. For so long he dreamed of this moment and now it was here. He gazed onto the harbor at the dhows, the dock workers loading and unloading the graceful ships, fishermen hawking their catch to eager buyers and the various other vendors crowding the busy seaport. He was so enamored with the scene that he didn't realize Fanus had entered his room until the old priest touched his shoulder.

Mikaili jumped then spun about, startled by his mentor. Fanus chuckled at him.

"Don't be so anxious," he said. "Once you have a taste of the sea your enthusiasm for it will quickly fade."

"I think not, Fanus," Mikaili said. "Ever since I've heard of the sea I wanted to ride upon its waves."

"Take it from an old man. Nothing is as it seems."

Fanus shuffled toward the door. "Get your things. Our dhow is leaving soon. Our nahoda is not a man that suffers tardiness well."

Mikaili collected his belonging from around the room then filled his packs. The other acolytes teased him for his messiness but Mikaili didn't care. He was the one chosen to accompany Fanus to Rome in order to re-establish relations between their worshippers and those to the north. It was an important task and his last test before becoming a priest.

He followed Fanus from the hostel, taking in the sights of the harbor town as they made their way to the harbor. It was so different from the quiet mountain town from where he hailed. The people of his home were dedicated to the life of the church; their routines revolved around the demands of the local temple. From the day he was born Mikaili was destined to be a priest. He would earn his robes then set out to establish his own church like his brothers before him. But first he would journey abroad, fulfilling a desire that long burned in his heart.

The nahoda of their dhow was as Fanus described. He scowled as they approached.

"The day is half gone!" he said. "We should be well on our way by now!"

Fanus grinned. "Never rush God's business, Abraha."

"This has nothing to do with God. You have always been late, Fanus!"

Mikaili moved closer to Fanus to whisper.

"You know him?"

Fanus nodded. "Abraha is an old friend. He hails from Axum as well, another lad who dreamed of the sea like you. Now he owns his own dhow which has made him cranky and smell of fish."

"Tardy priests and whispering apprentices make me cranky," Abraha said. He pointed a crooked finger at

Mikaili. "If you're going to talk about a man at least do so out loud."

Mikaili turned away, embarrassed. "I am sorry, elder. Forgive me of my sin."

Abraha huffed. "Just get on the dhow. We must depart while the wind still favors us."

The dhow set sail soon after everyone and everything was secure. Mikaili scurried about the deck, fascinated with every aspect of the vessel. He watched the baharia raise the lateen sail then studied how they maneuvered it to capture the wind. He was warned that the rocking of the ship on the sea might make him sick but Mikaili did not suffer such ills. Days into the journey he was still fresh, enjoying every experience with the exception of the food which was at most tolerable. Yet it didn't dampen his curiosity. One night as he rested on the deck he noticed Abraha working an interesting device while looking into the sky. He hurried to his side.

"Sir, what is it that you do?"

Abraha jerked his head, startled by Mikaili's sudden presence.

"What? Oh, it's you. You shouldn't sneak up on a man like that!"

"I'm sorry, sir. I'm curious about what you are doing?"

"I'm reading the stars and plotting our path," he said.

"Reading the stars?"

Abraha pointed into the sky. "The world changes, Mikaili. The stars don't. They look down on our useless souls indifferent to our plight. Some of them form patterns we call *kundinyota*. We know where these patterns are in the sky and we use them to plot our course."

"Teach me," Mikaili said.

"It's a waste of time," Abraha replied. "You're studying to be a priest. You'll have no need of such knowledge."

"Still, I would like to know," Mikaili said.

A slight smile came to Abraha's face. "I'll teach you on one condition."

Mikaili smiled. "What is that, sir?"

"That you pray for me," Abraha said. "I don't think God listens to me anymore."

"God always listens," Mikaili said. "But I'll be happy to add my prayers to yours."

Abraha nodded. "Let's get started then."

For the next few days Mikaili learned navigation from Abraha, seeking out the man after attending to Fanus's needs and his studies. He learned the names of the kundinyota and how to plot the course from their positions. Abraha's gruff demeanor faded; the nahoda actually seemed to look forward to their talks after a time. The journey was everything Mikaili imagined it would be.

"Fanus, Mikaili! Wake up!"

Mikaili rose from his cot then rubbed his eyes. A baharia loomed over him, his face filled with fear.

"What is it?" he said.

"*Maharimia!*"

Fanus sat upright.

"Maharimia? God protect us!"

The baharia hurried away. Mikaili jumped to his feet to follow but Fanus grabbed his wrist.

"Where are you going?"

"I'm going on deck to help."

"What can you do? You're not a fighter. You've never held a sword in your life."

Mikaili pulled away from Fanus.

"I can't wield a sword, but I can handle a staff. And if I can't fight, I can pray."

Fanus looked away, Mikaili sensing his shame.

"Teacher, I apologize if I..."

"Go," Fanus said.

Mikaili ran to the deck. The baharia worked the sail desperately while others looked to the horizon, swords and clubs in hand. Mikaili looked and saw the dhow approaching. He found Abraha standing at the stern, a grim look on his face. He looked at Mikaili.

"What are you doing here?"

"I came to help."

"The best way you can help is pray that they don't catch up with us. I've sailed these waters for countless seasons and not once have I encountered maharimia until now,' Abraha said. He reached out then grasped Mikaili's shoulder.

"I'm sorry your first voyage will end in such a way."

Mikaili tensed. Abraha did not believe they would survive the coming encounter.

"Give me a sword," he said.

Abraha shook his head. "They will surely kill anyone that fights them. You and Fanus stand a chance. You are priests. They may keep you alive out of respect or for ransom."

"Then you shouldn't fight either," Mikaili said.

Abraha sighed. "No, they will definitely kill me. I'm the nahoda."

Fear increased in Mikaili as the dhow came closer and closer. The maharimia hung from the ropes and stood on the bulwark, waving their sword and shouted obscenities at the merchant dhow. The dhows came closer; a group of the maharimia lifted crossbows and bows.

"Get down!" Abraha shouted.

The arrows and bolts rattled against the side of the dhow. Mikaili heard a scream then looked up to see a baharia writhing on the deck, and arrow protruding from neck. Their eyes met; Mikaili watched as life seeped from the hapless man, his fearful gaze transforming to an unfocused stare.

His bravery abandoned him. Mikaili prayed as he crawled across the deck then below to his room. Fanus knelt, praying incessantly. Mikaili joined him. The baharia would be no match for the maharimia; they had already lost the battle before the maharimia boarded. Only God could save them now.

The men fell against each other as the dhows smashed together. The deck erupted in the sounds of fighting men; clashing swords, tumbling bodies against the hard deck, shouts, cries and screams. Mikaili and Fanus prayed louder, desperate for divine intervention. The sounds of fighting diminished; the sound of footfalls replaced them as men clambered below deck. The footfalls ended before their door. Mikaili's faint hope of the baharia's victory died with the banging on the door. He stood then raised his staff. God would not save them this day, he decided. He would have to have himself.

The door crashed open and the maharimia poured in. Mikaili managed to strike the first maharimia in the head, sending him falling unconscious into his comrades. He tried to hit the second man but the wily maharimia grabbed his staff then jerked him forward. Mikaili braced himself for the sword he knew would soon pierce his body; instead the maharimia pulled him up to the deck, beating him along the way. They threw him down on the hard, blood slick deck before a pair of calloused sandaled feet.

"Here's the other one!"

Fanus groaned as he struck the deck beside him.

"Well, well, well," the man standing over them said. "Two priests in one day. We are the ones who are blessed!"

The gruff laughter stabbed Mikaili like a sword. God had deserted them.

"Stand up!" the man ordered.

Mikaili turned onto his stomach then pushed up to his knees. He grasped Fanus's arm then helped his mentor stand. The two of them looked down on the nahoda of the maharimia, a sun-kissed bearded man wearing a silken green robe and matching turban. He held a bloody shimsar in his right hand, a jagged dagger in his left. A jeweled jambiya rested in the red sash girding his waist. Mikaili glanced over the man's shoulder as tears welled in his eyes. Two of the maharimia dragged Abraha's body to the bulwark, lifted it over their heads then tossed it into the sea. He glared at the gaudy nahoda as his fingers curled into fists.

"Careful, priest," the nahoda said. "You could be joining them. As a matter of fact, that was my first notion. But I and my men live a dangerous life. We need someone to pray for us, and now we have two."

"I will not pray for sinners!" Fanus said.

The nahoda grinned. "So be it."

The nahoda drove his dagger into Fanus's stomach, twisted it then yanked it free. Mikaili caught his dying mentor then eased him to the deck. Fanus touched his cheek then managed to smile.

"It is God's will," he said. "Stay alive my son. Stay..."

Fanus closed his eyes then died.

Mikaili said a prayer over his mentor, letting the tears fall as spoke. Then he leapt to his feet, lunging at the nahoda. Once again, he expected to die; once again he was robbed of that peace. The nahoda struck him on the side of the head with his sword hilt. Mikaili sprawled onto the deck.

"Nice try, priest," he said. "I told you I needed a priest to pray for us. You'll do until I find another one."

The nahoda walked away.

"Shackle him then take him to our dhow with the booty. We're done here."

Mikaili stared at Fanus a moment a longer then turned away as the maharimia picked up his body. His captors dragged him over the plank then onto the maharimia dhow. The maharimia sacked the merchant dhow, bringing over valuables and dumping useless items and people over the side. After scouring the dhow, they set it afire, singing a vulgar song as they sailed away.

The maharimia dragged him to the mast then chained him to it. Mikaili slumped against it, his mind reeling. So much death in such a short time and he could do nothing to prevent it. He'd always questioned his faith and now his doubts were confirmed. He was not ready to be a priest; otherwise God would have prevented the maharimia from taking their ship. He watched the maharimia divide the spoils, fights breaking out between them as they determined who received what. A few of the fights were serious; at least two of the maharimia were killed during the harrowing negotiation. The nahoda received the majority of the spoils as apparently was his due. When all the loot had been divided the maharimia dispersed. The nahoda looked his way then grinned. Mikaili looked away then closed his eyes. Something metal rattled beside him and he opened his eyes. It was Abraha's navigation tool.

"A dying man's wish," the nahoda said.

Mikaili glared at the man.

"You honor his wish yet you kill him?"

The nahoda shrugged. "Honor among nahodas. He said you were a navigator, which is more valuable than a priest. It seems our navigator got himself killed during the boarding of your dhow. I told the greedy bastard to stay behind. He was a terrible swordsman, and now he's dead."

The nahoda nudged the instrument closer to Mikaili with his foot.

"There are maps below. After you're seasoned a bit I'll take you below then put you to work."

"Seasoned?" Mikaili said.

"You don't look like a person used to the sea. A few days on deck will remedy that. If you survive you'll be my navigator. Pray to your god for that."

Mikaili suffered for two weeks on the open deck. Some days the merciless sun scorched his skin; on other days he sat drenched from heavy rains. The maharimia fed him just enough to keep him alive, and what they did share with him was the worst of their provisions. During his seasoning he was forced to study the old navigator's maps. He gazed into the sky every night, struggling to decipher the kundinyota and wishing he could be among them as a spirit, free of the suffering. One night as he contemplated how he could end his life, a voice he thought he'd never hear again rang in his head.

"It is not His plan for you," Fanus said.

Mikaili sat up, hopeful energy fueling his movements.

"Fanus? Fanus! Where are you?" he said.

"I am dead," Fanus replied. "This you know."

"But you speak to me! How can this be? Am I dead too?"

"No, Mikaili. It is not your time."

Mikaili slumped against the mast. "Why do I suffer, Fanus? Why does He allow these terrible men to live?"

"I cannot comment on the fate of these men," Fanus said. "But for you, I will speak. It is a test of your faith, a moment that teaches you. You may not see so now, but you will."

"If I survive," Mikaili said.

Fanus did not reply.

The next day the nahoda came to the mast then released him.

"Your god favors you," he said. "Most men would be dead by now."

He handed Mikaili a new map.

"Take us to Salaht," he said. The nahoda strode away. Another man came to him carrying a bundle of clothes.

"Put these on," the man said. He dropped the garments on the deck.

Mikaili took a moment to massage his raw wrists and ankles then sifted through the clothes.

"These are the clothes of the dead," he said.

The man frowned. "What does it matter? They don't need them anymore."

Mikaili removed his ragged garment then put on the clothes. It was an ill fit, some too large, others too small, but it was better than the rags he's languished in for the past weeks.

The man studied him then nodded.

"You best get about your work," he said. "You have a strong heart but Saheed is still not certain about you. Do what he asks and he'll probably let you live."

"Living is no concern to me," Mikaili said. "If I die it is God's will. At least I'll be free of this suffering."

The man looked thoughtful for a moment then walked away.

Mikaili sat before the mast then began studying the maps. He did so the remainder of the day, attempting to correlate what he saw before him to where they were. It was fruitless. With no reference to land there was no way he could guide them anywhere. The nahoda, Saheed, approached him at dusk.

"Well?"

Mikaili looked up at the man, prepared for the worst.

"I have no idea where we are," he admitted. "I have no point of reference. We are surrounded by sea. I need to know where I am before I can tell you where we're going."

Saheed smiled. "You're learning."

He snatched the map from Mikaili's hand. He took out his knife then pricked his thumb; smearing his blood on the map then handing it back it back to Mikaili.

"That's where we are," he said. "Tonight, when the stars rise you should be able to plot our course. If you can't, you die."

Mikaili stood, no fear in his heart.

"And if I die, who will navigate?"

"I will," Saheed said. "I am capable but I prefer not to. I'm nahoda. Besides, a navigator gets the second largest cut of the booty we claim. It can be very good for you."

"I have no interest in your blood money," Mikaili said.

Pain blinded Mikaili as he fell to the deck. Saheed stood over him, rubbing his fist.

"Get it in your thick head that this is your life now, priest," he said. "The sooner you understand the longer you live."

Saheed took a sword and sheath from his waist belt then dropped in on the deck beside Mikaili.

"Learn how to use it," he said. "Everyone fights on my dhow."

Mikaili glared as he reached out then took the sword in his hands. Saheed grinned.

"I know what you're thinking, priest. You'd be dead before you got it out of the sheath. But when you think you're good enough you're welcomed to try. I don't deserve to be nahoda if I can't defeat you."

Saheed laughed as he walked away.

That night Mikaili read the stars. He used a candle to look at the map then back the glittering sky, marking his points with charcoal. He double checked his route before falling into a dreamless sleep. He was awakened the next morning by the same maharimia who brought him his food. The man waited while Mikaili cleared his bowl. He handed the bowl back but held onto it as the man grasped it.

"Who are you?" Mikaili said.

"Mussie," the man said.

"Why are you helping me? I know you don't have to do this."

The man looked about furtively before answering.

"Saheed's dhow is made of alliances," he said. "Everyone must have his friends."

"What makes you think I want to be your friend?"

"You have no choice if you want to live," Mussie said. "Like you I didn't ask to be here. I was captured from a grain barge. The others have been with the nahoda for many years. I survive because I'm good with a sword."

"But not as good as Saheed," Mikaili said.

Mussie grinned. "I think I am."

Mussie looked at the sword resting on his side.

"I will teach you. In return we will be allies. You will share your loot with me and you will pray for both of us."

Mikaili nodded.

"Where are we going?" Mussie asked.

"Salaht," Mikaili said.

A look of dread came to Mussie's face.

"We must get off this dhow before we reach that cursed place!"

"We can try," Mikaili said.

"There will be many docking between here and there. Salaht is on the other side of the world. It is a maharimia den; the strait is narrow and the shores wooded, a perfect place for maharimia to lie in wait."

Mikaili studied the map. "As soon as we reach here I will plot our course. Maybe we can escape at our first landing."

Mussie grinned. "Pray that we do."

The days crept by, Mikaili practicing with the sword during the day and navigating by night. Their first land fall was a small fishing village; the nahoda and a few of his trusted men went ashore to barter for fresh water and food, foiling any chances of escape. Their second landing was more promising. The city of Aden sprawled along its wide harbor, beckoning weary baharia as a respite from the sea. Mikaili's eyes gleamed as they approached the harbor, his excitement spurred by seeing this new city as much as by his possibility of losing himself in the throng. He approached Saheed as soon as they anchored.

"I need to go ashore," he said.

Saheed leaned against the bulwark, chewing on a betel leaf.

"For what?"

"I need more maps," he said. "I would also like to seek out someone with more knowledge of our routes."

"There are navigators in Aden," he said. "But I doubt they'll speak to you. They know what we are."

"I can try."

Saheed's eyes narrowed. "No. Tell Mussie what you need."

"I thought you said I was part of you crew. You treat me like a prisoner."

Saheed gave Mikaili another hard look then walked away. Mussie came to him soon afterwards.

"I'm sorry, Mikaili," he said. "We will have other chances."

They did not. Saheed refused to let Mikaili leave the dhow at every port, sending Mussie to gather anything he claimed to need. Their plan to escape came to an end as the narrow straits of Salaht came into view after months of sailing with the monsoons. Mussie visited him during the night.

"We have one more chance," he said. "Saheed is taking us to his city. Once we are there we can slip away into the jungle then make our way to the nearest port. Once we are there we can arrange passage to Vijayanagar."

Hope flared in Mikaili's heart for the first time in months.

"How soon will this occur?"

"Very soon," Mussie said. "We'll have to wait until the monsoons blow west."

"How long will that take?"

"Three months at least."

Mikaili's hope dampened. Three more months was an eternity which he wasn't sure he could survive.

"It seems a long time," Mussie said. "But it will pass quickly."

"I will trust you," Mikaili said.

The clanging of the muster bell broke their conversation. Saheed stood beside the bell ringer, his hands gripping his waist sash. Mikaili and the other gathered around with annoyed and curious expressions. When all had gathered the nahoda slapped the bell ringer across the back. The man glared at Saheed before ceasing.

"There's been a change of plans," Saheed said.

A collective groan passed through the maharimia.

"Word is that a vast fleet sails from the east from the Middle Kingdom. Now normally such a fleet would be invincible but the nahodas have agreed to put aside our rivalries for a chance at these riches. We are forming a fleet to meet this treasure fleet and take what we deserve!"

Saheed looked upon his men as if expecting an enthusiastic response. He received silence.

"Sounds like a big risk to me," one man said.

"I see nothing but death from this," another said.

"Seems to me the only maharimia that will profit from this is you," a third voice said.

"We're doing this whether you like it or not!" Saheed shouted. "Any man who wants off this dhow will have to go through me first!"

Mikaili's hand went to his sword.

"No," Mussie said. "You're not ready."

"Better die than continue this."

Mussie gripped Mikaili's wrist tight then forced his sword back into the scabbard.

"Trust me, brother. Now is not the time. Say you were lucky enough to kill Saheed. That would mean you could claim nahoda. But others would challenge you. You wouldn't survive the day."

"Navigator!"

A chill swept down Mikaili's spine as he looked up into Saheed's cold eyes. Had the nahoda seen his gesture and decided to call him out?

Mikaili walked forward, feeling the eyes of his crewmates. He halted before the nahoda.

"What do you wish?" he said.

A wicked smile came to Saheed's face.

"I wish you to pray for us," he said.

The crew broke into laughter. Saheed shoved a map into Mikaili's chest.

"These are the rendezvous points. You will get us to each one on time. Fail me once and you die."

Mikaili took the map then stomped away. He glared at Mussie as he took his place under the mast to study the map.

Over the next few weeks Mikaili guided the dhow to the rendezvous points. As they reached the final destination their numbers had swelled to thirty dhows in various stages of disrepair, a ragged fleet of nefarious purpose. The dhows then sailed east to meet the treasure fleet.

Mikaili stood on deck with the others, his eyes wide with fear. The treasure fleet approached through the narrow strait, protected by a vanguard of warships bristling with cannons and archers.

"We have sailed to our death," he whispered to Mussie.

"It seems so," Mussie said. "Let's see what our nahoda decides to do."

Saheed paced the deck, mumbling to himself as he worried his chin with his bejeweled right hand. He stopped then stomped his foot, cracking a plank.

"Where are they?" he said.

The warships sailed closer; soon they would be in cannon range. Though the maharimia fleet matched the treasure fleet in numbers, they were no match for the approaching ships. A frantic drum rhythm carried over the waters, causing Saheed to clinch his fists.

"No! No!" he shouted.

The maharimia dhows broke formation, each sailing in different directions. A decision had been made and conveyed by the drums; the treasure fleet was too strong to attack.

"Fools!" Saheed shouted.

Mikaili broke his silence.

"What do we do nahoda?"

Saheed jerked his head toward Mikaili.

"We stay, sea priest," he said.

"We'll be in cannon range soon," Mikaili said.

"Don't you think I know that? Be quiet and tend to the wheel!"

A commotion on the shores caught Mikaili's attention. Hundreds of men appeared on the jungle edge, carrying long wide boats. They dropped the boats into the water, boarded then rowed toward the treasure fleet, chanting in a language strange to Mikaili's ears.

"Aha!" Saheed said.

The warships veered away from maharimia fleet. The boatmen raised shields, protecting themselves from showers of crossbow bolts and arrows fired from the treasure dhows. Once they reached the ships long bamboo poles rose from the boats, slamming against the bulwark. The half-naked boatmen swiftly scrambled up the poles with knives clenched between their teeth then swarmed onto the ships.

The maharimia dhows turned again toward the treasure ships, taking advantage of the boatmen's distraction. Saheed pointed at a treasure ship breaking formation.

"That one!" he shouted. "Take us to that one!"

Mikaili steered the dhow toward the treasure ship.

"The rest of you get below to the oars!" he yelled.

Half the crew rushed below then manned the oars. The dhow lurched forward under their efforts. Those remaining on deck climbed the mast with their bows while others crowded the bulwark with grappling ropes and hooks. A weak volley of arrows fell on the dhow; the maharimia jeered the hapless sailors of the treasure ship as the gap between the vessels narrowed.

The grappling ropes flew as Mikaili guided the dhow parallel to the treasure ship. Archers released their arrows, peppering the ill prepared crew. The maharimia laughed as the men died, pulling harder on the ropes and dragging the treasure ship close. The crafts crashed together; Mikaili stumbled with the impact. A strong hand gripped his collar then steadied him. He turned to look into Saheed's face.

"Come, sea priest," he said. "It's time to claim you pay!"

Saheed dragged Mikaili to the boarding plank then pushed him over into the treasure boat. Mikaili fell into chaos. Maharimia and baharia fought around him, clashing metal filling his ears. He drew his sword, his eyes locked on Saheed as the nahoda cut and slashed his way through the treasure ship defenders. Now was the time to kill him; in the confusion of the boarding no one would notice. He prayed for strength as he stepped over the dead and dying, coming closer and closer to the foul man.

"Ahhh!"

Mikaili turned instinctively to his left then raised his sword to guard position. It met the desperate swing of the mad baharia attacking him, the man's forehead bleeding from a cut at his hairline. The man's attack was skilled and relentless, driving Mikaili further and further away from Saheed. He could no longer think of Saheed; he had to save his own life. He blocked and parried the best he could, occasionally seeing an opportunity to take the man's life but he refused. He was a priest, not a killer.

His back slammed against the bulwark. Mikaili dodged the man's thrust but was not fast enough to evade his punch. Bright pain blinded him; he struck back with his sword. When his vision cleared he saw his assailant staggering away holding his stomach, dark blood seeping between his fingers. The man looked down at his wound, then back at Mikaili.

"Maharimia bastard!" he said.

He swayed, collapsed to the deck, and then died.

Mikaili stared at him as the battle subsided. He dropped his sword, fell to his knees then tried to pray. The words stuck in his throat. He opened his eye to look upon the man he killed. The man's words were true. He was no priest. He was a maharimia.

He stood then went to the man's body. Mikaili knelt beside him. He took the man's ring, a simple band of gold. He took the copper necklace around his neck and the dagger from his hip. The last thing he took was the man's sword. When he stood he looked into Mussie's face.

"You're one of us now," Mussie said.

"Yes I am," Mikaili replied.

They grabbed what loot they could, set the treasure ship afire then boarded their dhow. Fortune was with them; the warships were so occupied with saving the larger ships they were are able to slip away almost unnoticed. The alliance between the maharimia quickly dissolved and they found themselves pursued by dhows that were allies moments ago. Mikaili manned the wheel, combining his navigation skills and a good wind to outpace them. He sailed the ship from the narrow strait to the open water. Once he was sure they were clear of pursuers they dropped anchor. The maharimia gathered on deck, depositing their loot into a pile. Saheed was the first to step forward, taking his choice from the booty. His arms full, he looked at Mikaili.

"Claim your prize," he said with a wicked grin. "You earned it."

Mikaili picked through the pile. There was no smile on his stricken face. This was a memorial to those who died defending it. He felt like a violator, not a victor. Still he had no right to judge. He added to the pile; he added to the dead as well.

He searched the pile until he found the items he claimed from the man he murdered. It was all he took. The other maharimia grinned; Saheed frowned.

"Think hard, sea priest," he said. "This is all you'll get."

Mikaili glared at Saheed. "It's all I want."

After the others divided the spoils Mikaili was given a small cabin, the dwelling of the former navigator. The room was musty and filthy but much better than living on deck. He cleaned it as best he could then settled into the worn hammock. Someone knocked on his door and he grabbed his dagger.

"Come in," he said.

Mussie entered, his hands full with necklaces and other jewelry.

"That was foolish," he said.

Mikaili put down the dagger then lay on the hammock.

"I desired nothing," he said.

"You don't understand," Mussie replied. "Saheed supported you until now. You are one of us now; you earn you own keep. We'll trade what we claim at the next port for food, clothes and other needs. If you don't get it yourself, you won't have it. Understand?"

Mikaili rose from the hammock and accepted Mussie's offering.

"When do we leave?" he said.

"It will be a while yet," Mussie said. "The treasure fleet has scattered. Saheed want to hunt those down that he can. Once we've done so we'll sail for his city."

"His city?"

Mussie nodded. "It is the other reason he wished to sail east. We must be gone by then."

"We will be," Mikaili replied.

The next few weeks were spent crisscrossing the straits, chasing down the remnants of the hapless treasure fleet. Mikaili became a killer, boarding with the other maharimia, killing when he had to then gathering the spoils of his grim work. He gained the respect of the other maharimia, but it was admiration he despised. Every day pushed him farther and farther away from what he meant to be. The others still called him Sea Priest and Saheed forced him to pray for them. But they were empty prayers. God did not exist on this dhow.

After weeks of pillaging the sea Saheed ordered Mikaili to take them to Salaht. It was a ragged, filthy place, a patchwork of building and huts rimming the broad bay. A crowd gathered at the dilapidated mooring, hungry eyes fixed on the lone vessel. Saheed went to the bow then cupped his hands over his mouth. He spoke a language Mikaili didn't recognize; the crowd cheered in response, waving their hands over their heads.

He strode to Mikaili.

"Welcome home, priest," he said. "I won't need your services for a time. You're a decent navigator so I won't kill you. At least not now."

The maharimia disembarked, wading into the receptive throng. Mikaili watched, longing for the familiar sights of his homeland. But that was not to be. A hand on his shoulder broke his musing.

"Don't worry," Mussie said. "Our chance is near. Just be patient."

"I'll try," Mikaili whispered.

Mikaili followed the others into the maharimia port. The deeper they went, the more depressing the surroundings. It was a squalid town, filled with folk that seem to hang onto existence with blind tenacity. Everyone followed Saheed to the town center where the items not claimed by the crew were distributed among the city inhabitants. A few fights broke as people scrambled for goods; Mikaili watched as a throng of women and children surrounded the vile nahoda.

"Priest!" he called out. "You will reside with me. I need to keep you close."

Mikaili glanced at Mussie as he trudged to Saheed's side.

"This place is a cesspool," Mikaili said.

"I would take that as an insult if it wasn't true," Saheed said. "One day it will be a great city, one that will rival Beijing, Vijayanagar and Mombasa."

Saheed reached into his pocket. "By the way, I have something for you."

The maharimia nahoda extracted a Coptic cross.

"For you."

Mikaili punched Saheed in the face. His sword was in his hand as the nahoda fell. Saheed rolled, barely avoiding Mikaili's blade then climbing to his feet, his back to the raging priest. Mikaili slashed and Saheed cried out as Mikaili's blade sliced across his back. Saheed spun about, his blade in his hand.

"Die, priest!" he yelled.

If Saheed's skills were legendary Mikaili did not notice. The men fought like crazed beasts, stabbing, slashing and hacking each other with no regard for themselves. Mikaili clothes clung to his body, pasted to his skin with sweat and blood. Though weak, Saheed's visage fueled him on. The others ringed around them, yelling encouragement and placing bets as the men attempted to kill each other. Darkness attempted to overwhelm Mikaili but he pushed it away. He would not fall before Saheed. He would not stop until the vile nahoda lay dead at his feet.

Saheed's angry expression changed into one of surprise. He shuddered then fell. Standing behind him with a bloody blade was Mussie.

"Run, Mikaili!" Mussie shouted.

Mikaili stumbled away. He swung his sword at the maharimia blocking his way and they stepped aside, their faces still stunned. He had no idea where he was going; he just had to get away. The city dwindled away as he neared the surrounding jungle; soon he struggled down a narrow trail. His legs finally failed him and he fell in the middle of the trail.

Hands grasped his arms then dragged him into the foliage. He heard voices he didn't recognize as he was dragged deeper into the bush. His head struck something hard and he blacked out.

When he awoke Mussie squatted beside him. A fire burned, its weak light struggling against the night. A small animal roasted over the flames on a makeshift spit. Mussie sliced a strip of meat from the carcass then handed it to him. Mikaili took the meat then ate it. It was bland but nourishing.

"Where are we?" he asked.

"In the jungle," Mussie replied.

"Are they after us?"

Mussie cut the leg from the animal. "Not yet. They're too busy fighting over who should be nahoda. I'm not sure if they will come after us."

They sat in silence, eating their meager meal.

"That was a foolish thing to do," Mussie said.

"It had to end," Mikaili said. "Either his life or mine. I couldn't stand it any longer."

"It would have been your life if I had not stepped in," Mussie said.

"I guess I should thank you," Mikaili said.

"You can thank me when we're free of this place. Rest now. We have a hard day tomorrow."

The next day they began the long walk to the sea. Mikaili slowly recovered with each day which allowed him to help with gathering food. When the sound of the surf finally reached their ears, they ran recklessly to its source, emerging from the stifling jungle to the bare sandy shores.

"Now that we are here, what do we do?" Mikaili said.

"I don't know," Mussie replied.

Mikaili looked out into the ocean then up into the blue, cloud specked sky.

"We don't want to head west," he said. "That will take us back to Saheed. We should follow the shore east. If we are lucky we'll come across another harbor town. If we're not, then we'll be a village of two."

Mussie laughed. "There is still humor inside you. That's good."

Mikaili managed a smile. "Not much else."

"Pray for us," Mussie said. "We'll need it."

Mikaili's smile faded. He began walking to the west, Mussie close behind. He had no idea what they would find but he was certain of one thing. There was no faith in his heart. He would never be a priest.

MWANAMKE TEMBO (THE ELEPHANT WOMAN)

For six months of the year Kiswahili, Arab and Indian ships sailed west with the monsoons, their dhows pregnant with the goods of East Africa. Six months later they returned, their African bounty exchanged for eastern luxuries and ready to begin the cycle again. Belay played both sides of the coin like most Swahili traders. One particular item whose value spread beyond Africa was ivory. The tusks of the massive tembos were prized throughout the trade lands for its beauty and versatility. It was a common item of trade, its value fluctuating with supply and demand. This particular season ivory was invaluable for it was nowhere to be found.

Changa assisted the other baharia making repairs on Belay's dhows when the messenger boy found him. The boy trembled as he took in the imposing presence that was Changa Diop, former pit fighter now merchant apprentice.

"Changa, bwana Belay wishes to see you immediately!"

Changa nodded then sauntered to Yusef, who sat on the docks raising his gourd to his lips. Changa slapped the container from his hand.

"Come with me" he ordered.

"Where are we going?" Yusef slurred.

"To see Belay. Pretend you're sober."

They accompanied the boy to Belay's house near the docks.

They followed the boy to Belay's home. The old merchant paced the floor in the lower level, mumbling as he was prone to do when he was agitated.

"Bwana, you sent for me?"

Belay jerked his head toward Changa and smiled.

"Ah, Changa! Come, I have a special task for you."

Belay's smile dissipated when he noticed Yusef barely standing.

"Is he drunk?"

"No, bwana," Yusef slurred.

"Get out!" Belay shouted.

Yusef bowed and almost fell into Belay. Changa caught his big friend and spun him towards the door.

"Wait for me outside," he whispered.

Belay glared at Yusef until he exited.

"I would toss him into the streets if it wasn't for you," he said. "Why do you tolerate him?"

Changa shrugged. "He's a good man. You won't find a harder worker or more loyal man in Mombasa."

"When he's not in trouble," Belay added. He sat at his desk. "I need you to take a safari into the interior. The

Omani want ivory and there is none. My contacts are very late."

"How soon do I need to leave?"

"As soon as possible," Belay replied. "If they can't get ivory from me they'll sail down the coast."

"I'll make arrangements immediately," Changa said as he stood.

Belay came to him, placing a fatherly hand on his shoulder. "Do not fail me, Changa."

Changa returned the gesture. "I won't, bwana."

Changa was ready to depart within a week. His crew consisted of eighty men, sixty bearers and twenty warriors. They departed at first light, making good time despite their provisions and trade goods. Belay had given Changa much responsibility on the safari, more than he'd done in the past. He had the merchant's permission to trade for the precious material at the hunting camps. It was a test of Changa's skill and he was eager for the opportunity.

The safari also offered a useful reason for Yusef's participation. Changa's looming friend was Kikuyu and knew the way to the tembo hunting camps. It saved them the expense of hiring a guide, which thrilled Belay immensely. The bulky man stood before the group, his fists pressed into his hips, a scowl on his face.

"Come on, dogs!" he shouted. "The sun slips away. We have miles to cover and ivory to claim!"

Changa smirked as he shook his head. "Calm down, Yusef. These men are porters, not slaves."

Yusef huffed. "I've seen better men buried under vultures."

"Grab your gear and let's go," Changa said. "Like you said, the sun slips away."

The safari began mid-morning and did not go unnoticed. Any plan by Belay drew attention. His domain was the sea, so the inland excursion drew much curiosity. After a brief stop on the mainland to secure additional supplies, they entered the mainland. Years had passed since Changa journeyed inland and he was overwhelmed by the plethora of wildlife inhabiting the savannah. Yusef strode ahead, a huge smile on his face. He turned to Change with sparking eyes.

"This is my home, kibwana. This is the land that made me." He slowed, walking stride for stride with Changa.

"I'm saving my coins to purchase one hundred head of cattle and one hundred bushels of sorghum to plant my fields. I'll build a farm outside my home village. When I become wealthy I will take many wives from the best families who will bear me sons."

"That's a bold future coming from a man who loves palm wine as much as you."

"Make fun of me while you can, kibwana," Yusef said. "I would break your thin neck if I didn't have so much respect for you."

Changa laughed. "Lucky for me. Just keep focused on our task."

They came across the first village two days later. The chief, Kiamboga, was a short, thick man with bulbous cheeks. He offered them food and rest, but Changa's impatience would not allow it.

"We seek the tembo hunters," Changa said.

The chief nodded. "As do we. In normal years our men would travel to Mombasa with tusks from the hunters. They are not farmers so they trade us for food, milk and meat. But they have not come. The men we sent to contact them have not returned."

"You have no idea what happened to them?" Changa asked.

Kiamboga shook his head. "Like I said, we are not hunters. They could have been killed by Maasai or lions. Who knows? Their families mourn and I can do nothing. We will send no more men. The money we make from the tusks is good but not necessary."

"Is there someone that could lead us to the hunters?" Yusef asked.

"Of course," Kiamboga answered. "But they won't. You are a good group of warriors but my people are tired of disappearing."

"I will show you."

Changa and the others sought the owner of the female voice that volunteered. She knelt, her head partially bowed as he looked at them. Wide brown eyes scanned them then lingered on Changa. She lifted her head, exposing her plain and determined face to all.

"This is not your place," Kiamboga said to the woman.

"My husband is gone," she countered. "If you will not find him I will."

She strode to Changa. "I am Kenda. I will take you to the tembo hunters."

"No!" Kiamboga protested. "You will bring her wrath on us, too?"

Changa placed a puzzled gaze on the chief. "Her? Kiamboga, what is going on here?"

Kiamboga glared at Kenda before responding. "The people call her Mwanamke Tembo, the elephant woman. They say she is the reason the ivory has stopped. Some say she has killed the hunters because they slaughter her children."

Changa frowned skeptically. "And you believe this?"

Kiamboga shrugged. "All I know is the ivory supply has ceased and my men have not returned."

"Maybe there is war in the interior," Yusef offered.

"That could be," Changa answered. "It wouldn't be the first time a war interrupted good trade. Still, bwana Belay has given us a task and we must complete it."

Changa extended his hand to the chief. "Thank you for your hospitality. I hope you don't mind if we allow Kenda to help us."

Kiamboga waved his hand. "It's her fate, not mine. Not that I expect anything to happen to you, bwana Changa."

Changa chuckled. "Of course, you don't."

He left the village and set up camp. By nightfall they cooked over the campfires. Kenda sat at Changa's fire, her sad eyes gazing into the flames. Yusef plopped down beside her, a gourd of palm wine in his large hands.

"What troubles you, sister?" he asked.

Kenda's head snapped in his direction. "What do you think? My husband is missing two weeks now. I cannot manage our farm myself. I must find him."

"Who manages it now?" Yusef asked. "You husband is gone and you are here. What about your children?"

Kenda slapped the wine gourd from Yusef's hand. "If I cannot find my husband I can't keep my farm. My children and I will starve. If Kiamboga wont' find him, I will."

"Your husband may be dead, Kenda," Changa said. "We won't know until we find the tembo hunters."

"Changa!" Yusef exclaimed. "Your words are harsh."

Changa shrugged. "There's no need to lie. Kenda knows this. That's why she's here."

Changa looked at the woman. Her wet eyes reflected the firelight as he turned away. Yusef frown at him.

"We cannot be sure," he said.

Kenda stood and stalked away from the fire. Changa went back to enjoying his stew, ignoring Yusef's angry stare.

"You didn't have to say that," Yusef said.

"She knows," Changa answered. "That's why she's here. Either we will find him ore we won't."

Kenda led them through the scrub forests and open land, setting a pace that was difficult to maintain for men used to dhow life. They spent the night at the base of a wooded ridge, the men grateful, Kenda disappointed. The next day they scaled the hill.

"The hunters' camp is over the ridge," she said.

They reached the summit by midday. Below them was the camp, or what remained of it. The huts were crushed, piles of grass and thatch surrounded by decaying bodies. Kenda let out a painful wail and scrambled down the hill. Changa and his men followed more cautiously. They wandered among the destruction, their weapons at the ready.

"Something definitely happened here," Changa said.

"The hunters lost," Yusef said.

"Search the camp. Check the perimeter for tracks. Whoever did this much destruction had to leave a trail."

"Are we going to fight them," Yusef asked.

"Of course not," Changa said. "I want to know how long ago this took place. Whoever did this might return."

"Bwana, come quickly!"

Changa ran to the excited porter. He and three others gestured at a large ruin. Protruding from the pile were the tips of tusks. Changa moved aside the grass, exposing a wealth of ivory.

"It seems we have been blessed," he announced. "Whoever destroyed the camp didn't do it for wealth. They would have taken the tusks."

"It was probably Maasai," Yusef said. "They care for nothing but cattle."

"Whatever the reason, there's more than enough for us to take back. We'll make camp in the hills just in case whoever did this returns."

Yusef gestured towards Kenda. She trudged to each body, kneeling before it and inspecting it delicately with her fingers, her lips moving with silent words.

"She won't find him," Changa said. "Even if he's here she won't recognized him. They've been dead too long."

"Maybe see can sense him," Yusef replied. "He was her husband. They say that a woman and her husband have a special bond. "We should help her."

"You can help her," Changa suggested. "I came here to find ivory and I have."

"We would not have found it without her," Yusef argued.

Changa folded his arms across his chest. "That's true, but like I said, there is nothing we can do."

Yusef went to Kenda and stood beside her. She glanced at him then continued her morbid inspection. Changa and the others went into the hills to set up camp. By nightfall they had eaten and retired to their tents. Sleep came quickly to Changa, pleased that he'd completed his first task for Belay so quickly.

Changa awoke suddenly; his hands seeking his sword. A feeling had seeped into his mind, the sense that something was coming, something ominous. Moments later the ground trembled beneath him. He jumped to his feet as the trembling increased. A sound ripped through the night, a sharp trumpeting that gripped his heart and pressed out a hint of fear. He came out of his hut and was greeted by the fearful eyes of his companions. Yusef rambled to him.

"The ground shakes, kibwana," he said. "It happens here sometimes."

Changa didn't reply. His attention was drawn to a wavering luminescence rising over the horizon. The trembling grew as the light came closer. The trumpeting increased, a sound heavy with warning.

"Tembo," one porter said. "Something has frightened them."

"Or angered them," Changa added.

"Where is Kenda?" Yusef asked.

Changa scanned the camp. The woman was nowhere to be seen. Yusef must have done the same; for no sooner had Changa looked at his friend did he rush down the hill to the hunters' camp. Changa chased after him, followed by the rest of the men. The strange light increased, beams streaking through the trees and illuminating the camp.

Changa emerged from the tree line and stumbled. A ragged vanguard of tembos advanced on the camp. But these beasts were like nothing he'd ever seen.

Bleached bones showed through their translucent hides, their trunks ghostly extensions from their heads. They followed the largest tembo, a massive matriarch whose trunk emitted the eerie blasts cutting through the humid night. Astride her was a woman. Tribal patterns laced her face, lines that glowed with the spectral light of the herd. The tembo rider held a massive shoka (axe) in her left hand. She waved the weapon while screaming a sound similar to the matriarch.

Kenda stood before the charging herd, her face bunched in anger. She yelled at the herd, her voice drowned by their cacophonous stampede. The tembos stopped before her, rising in unison on their hind legs. Yusef reached the woman and lifted her into his arms like

an errant child. The tembo rider leaped from the matriarch, the shoka raised high as she dropped like a bird of
prey towards Yusef and Kenda. Changa passed the fleeing
duo, raising his sword and knife above his head. The rider
slammed into the three of them, pitching Yusef and Kenda
forward. Change caught the massive blade between his
blades as he fell onto his back. He stared into the malevolent eyes of the tembo woman. Her skin was grey like the
ghostly animals she commanded, hanging loosely from
her gaunt frame. She pressed the shoka down, the blade
inching closer to his face. Changa had fought many unnatural adversaries but never had he experienced such relentless strength. This was a struggle he was sure to lose.
Changa let his arms go limp as he jerked his head aside.
The blade plunged into the ground inches from his face.
He twisted his body, throwing the tembo woman aside.
She rolled and sprang to her feet before Changa. She
snatched her shoka free and attacked him again. Changa
rolled and blocked, desperate for a chance to stand. The
tembo woman was too fast.

The woman raised her shoka again and Changa heard
a familiar yell. Yusef crashed into her and the two tumbled
away. Yusef's advantage was temporary. A grey trunk
struck him like a serpent, wrapping around his thick waist
and tossing him aside like a twig. Yusef's diversion did
give Changa time to stand but nothing more. No sooner
had he regained his feet did the woman attack again. Her
ghostly pachyderms attacked with her, flailing their trunks

at him. Changa withstood the relentless pummeling as he concentrated on avoiding the woman's sinister shoka.

A roar split the ominous night and the tembos answered, trumpeting as they fell away. A simba leapt into Changa's sight, a full mane feline larger than any he'd seen. It drove the tembos back, swiping at their legs and trunks with no sign of fear. Changa raise his dented sword to deflect another shoka swing and was shoved to the ground. He looked up to see a different woman standing over him brandishing two swords.

"Nokofa!" she shouted. "This is not your realm!"

Nokofa, the tembo woman, backed away.

"Shangé?" Her eyes narrowed and she snarled.

"So, they send the fallen one to do their dirty work. You cannot help them. They would hunt until my children were no more. I will not allow that."

Nokofa raised her head and trumpeted. Her tembos gathered behind her. She leaped backwards, landing on the head of the matriarch. Nokofa trumpeted again and the herd disappeared into darkness.

Changa finally had a moment for the strangeness of the night to settle. The lion strolled up to the woman called Shangé, nuzzling against her thigh. She sheathed her swords and embraced the simba, her arms disappearing in his thick mane. She closed her eyes and smiled.

"Thank you," Changa said.

The woman stood suddenly and the simba crouched.

"No, Mijoga!" she ordered. Her eyes narrowed on Changa.

"Leave now before Nokofa returns," she said.

"We came for the tusks," Changa replied.

"Leave them. Nokofa will kill you if you touch them."

Changa hesitated, considering his words before answering.

"We can't," he finally said. "We came for the tusks and we won't leave without them."

"Then she will kill all of you," Shangé said. She turned to walk away but Changa grabbed her shoulder.

"Wait," he began.

Shangé slapped his hand away. Mijoga ambled towards him, a low rumble seeping from his bared teeth.

"Leave this place," she warned again. "Never come back."

Shangé and Mijoga strode into the darkness. Changa watched them disappear, his mind a jumble of thoughts until a familiar moan reached his ears.

"Yusef!"

The burly Kikuyu lumbered out the darkness supported by two comrades. Kenda walked beside him, her eyes staring into his.

"Are you okay?" Changa asked.

Yusef nodded then grimaced. "I'll be better in the morning. What just happened? We have intruded on a battle between spirits it seems."

"We know why the ivory has stopped," Changa said. "The tembo woman has declared war on the hunters."

"So we go home empty handed," Yusef concluded. "Belay will not be happy."

"Neither am I." Changa's face mirrored his disappointment.

"We'll rest tonight," he said. "Tomorrow I'll decide what we do."

The strange encounter did nothing to affect the camp's slumber. Snores, grunts and heavy breathing joined the sounds of night beasts among the dark hills and grassland. There was no such comfort for Changa. He sat at the fire, the glowing embers casting a faint light on his brooding visage. He wished a war had been the reason for the ivory shortage. In war there was always someone more interested in themselves, some person willing to look the other way for the right price. But spirits had no price; they fought for their own reason, motives far beyond the comprehension of men. He would have to find a way to circumvent Nokofa's anger and Shangé's warning. He had to get those tusks.

Something moved just beyond Changa's vision. He jumped to his feet, a throwing knife in his hand. Two figures emerged from the darkness, both unconcerned with his stance. Shangé and Mijoga had returned.

"There is no way around this," Shangé said. "You must leave."

"I won't leave without ivory," Changa stated. "Why should Nokofa or you care? The tembos are dead. Why should it matter if we take the ivory?"

"Because if you return the others will want more and the hunters will return," Shangé said.

"You agree with Nokofa?"

Shangé sat before the embers. Mijoga lay beside her, resting his massive head against her.

"I do not care about the fate of the tembos. But Nokofa lives for them. She is their totem spirit, the master of the place where their spirits rests. She has heard their stories of the hunters and it has angered her. She came to stop the killing, but that is not her place."

Shangé stared at Changa and he shifted. She seemed to be inspecting him, contemplating.

"Since you will not leave maybe you can help me."

Changa was intrigued. "How?"

"I cannot defeat Nokofa alone. Mijoga is a noble companion but her tembos are too many. You and your friend may help reduce the odds."

Changa smirked. "Nokofa almost killed me."

"A lesser warrior would be dead," Shangé replied. "As for your friend, he's not as skilled as you, but he is durable. He may live long enough for us to succeed."

Sunlight brushed the eastern horizon with a reddish-yellow hue. Shangé glanced at the dawn and stood. "I will not force you to do this. If you wish your ivory meet me before the hunters' camp at midday."

She reached into the edge of her waist and extracted a small bag. She extended to Changa and their hands touched. Shangé's eyes widened, a smile coming to her face like the rising sun.

"It seems you hold your own secrets," she said. "The son of a kabaka is no ordinary man. You will make a strong ally."

Shangé's words distracted Changa, sending him back to a time he'd buried away. There was not time for memories; he had to concentrate on the task at hand.

"What is this?" he asked.

"Boil this and use it to clean your blades. It will help you against the tembo spirits."

Shangé and Mijoga melded into the bush. Moments later the camp stirred. Yusef came to him, the big man rubbing the sleep from his eyes.

"Kibwana, did you sleep well?"

"I don't know," Changa replied. He looked at his hand; he still held the herb bag, a confirmation that Shangé's visit was not a dream.

"We should go home," Yusef advised. "The tembo woman will not let us collect the ivory and we are too few to hunt for it ourselves."

"I won't go home empty-handed," Changa countered. "Take this bag and boil the contents. Once it is ready we'll wash our weapons with it."

Changa handed Yusef the bag. Yusef looked at it suspiciously.

"Just do as I say," Changa scolded.

While the others went about their day, Changa waited for Shangé. He wondered how she knew of his past just by a touch and why it mattered. He was far away from that life, unable to return. Usenge took his father's life and sent him fleeing, his ruthless tebos hunting him for years. Yes, he was the son of a kabaka, but it had done him no good. He could never stand against Usenge, at least not alone.

When he was young he vowed to return to Kongo, avenge his father's murder and free his mother and sisters from Usenge. But as a man he realized what a foolish dream it was. It was best to bury those memories and get on with his new life, which it was important to return with the tusks.

Shangé and Mijoga emerged from the bush at midday. Yusef and the others rushed to Changa's side, weapons ready. He waved them down.

"Who is that?" Yusef asked. "Another spirit?"

"No," Changa replied. "They are here to help us. Nafasi!"

A short muscular man with round cheeks and a serious face stepped forward.

"You're in charge until we return. Don't go into the camp."

"How long shall we wait for you?" Nafasi asked.

"Two weeks." It was a guess at the most.

Nafasi nodded and went back to his duties. Yusef and Changa ambled down the hill to Shangé. The woman looked them over and nodded her approval.

"It will take a week to reach Nokofa's refuge. I trust you told your people to stay away from the camp?"

"I did."

"Good, let's go." Shangé patted Mijoga's head and they jogged into the bush. Changa and Yusef followed. They ran the remainder of the day, stopping only when darkness demanded it. Shangé built a fire while Changa and Yusef rested, both men exhausted. Mijoga loped off into the darkness, returning later with an antelope between his jaws. He dropped the carcass and waited patiently as Shangé cut a section for the four of them. The largest portion she gave back to the simba. They cooked the meat over the fire and ate silently. Changa stared at Shangé, wondering if he should ask the questions worrying him. She looked up suddenly and smiled.

"Ask your questions, merchant man," she said.

"Why is Mwanamke Tembo killing the hunters?"

"Because they kill her spirit-children."

"Then she is a tembo," Yusef concluded.

"No, she's not," Shangé said. "She is the spirit that watches over them. She maintains the balance. The hunters were taking too many so she stopped them."

"And by doing so upset the balance," Changa surmised.

Shangé nodded. "This is why I must stop her."

"Are you a spirit?" Yusef asked.

Shangé smiled sadly. "Not anymore. I serve those who rule over us all."

Mijoga appeared. He lay before Shangé and licked his paws. Shangé massaged his mane and her purred.

"I was once like her," she said. "Man was my charge and I watched over them dutifully. Like Nokofa I came to care for them too much. A certain man drew my special attention, the son of a chief whose spirit glowed like my own. One day he looked up into the stars and stared into my eyes as if he knew I watched him. He was so handsome; his body was strong like a baobab. His name was Mijoga."

Changa's eyes shifted to the magnificent simba. Mijoga glanced at Shangé and licked his paws.

"One day Mijoga looked up into the sky and called for me," Shangé continued. A little smile formed on her face. "I answered. We loved under the stars, exposed to the eyes of my own. No sooner did we touch that I was taken away from him. We were judged and condemned. Mijoga was to be killed; his soul cast into darkness, but my mother, spirit of the lions, intervened. She placed his essence into the body of a simba. I was stripped of my status, cast to the world as mortal. Though we were separated we eventually found each other."

"So why do you serve those who condemned you and your lover?" Yusef asked.

Shangé's expression was mixed. "Because it is all I know. I still hope that I will be forgiven. I may not rise again among the spirits, but they may at least grant Mijoga back his life. That would be enough."

They ran the next two days in tense silence, Changa barely noticing the change in landscape. Scrub brush and grasses melded into rocky soil and hills pockmarked by shallow lakes. They covered less ground, slowed by the taxing terrain. On the fourth day Shangé finally broke the silence over a meal of wildebeest and yams.

"We are close," she announced. "We will attack at dusk. She will be at her weakest then."

"Why?" Changa asked.

"Nokofa cannot sustain her nyama all day. During the day her tembos sleep. She summons them at dusk."

Changa nodded as he chewed his yam.

"You and I will confront her directly," she continued. "Yusef and Mijoga will deal with the tembos."

Yusef stopped chewing his meal, his mouth dropping open. "You want me to fight a tembo?"

"They are spirits. The require Nokofa's nyama to exist. They will be weak at the most. Besides, you'll have Mijoga with you."

The simba growled at the mention of its name. It looked at Yusef with assurance in its eyes. Yusef looked back, shaking his head. Changa was concerned as well but he had no choice. They had to trust Shangé.

"How will we do this?" he asked. "She is hard to kill."

"We can't kill her. She is immortal."

"So, what do we do?"

"Nokofa wears a talisman that gives her human form. If we can take it from her she will revert to a spirit. She won't be able to harm us or them."

So, there was a chance, Changa thought. "What it this talisman?"

"It is the leopard band around her head. It contains the gris-gris securing her in this world."

After another day of travel, they arrived in Nokofa's realm. Tall trees grew thick in the ash fed soil, blanketing mounds of earth that once spewed fire. Shangé stopped and shaded her eyes. She pointed to a cluster of stooped hill, each identical in height and width.

"There," Shangé said. "We'll find Nokofa beyond those hills."

Changa rubbed his chin to hide his unease. He recalled his last encounter with the tembo woman. Yusef looked at him, his eyes worried.

"We should rest," Shangé finally said. "We'll need all our strength tonight."

Changa did not sleep and neither did Shangé. He watched her pace before the fire, her eyes watching the outline of the hills against the clear night sky. Occasionally she would peer at the heavens, her mouth moving but emitting no sound. Changa wasn't sure, but it seemed the stars shifted in response. He closed his eyes and tried to sleep. All he wanted was to bring back the ivory back to Mombasa.

Shangé roused them as soon as the sun descended below the hills. They climbed together, tracing a winding path to the hilltops. A pale-yellow glow radiated over the mounds, pulsing in time with a rhythmic voice rising over the trees. Dozens of feet below them a bizarre scene played out. Nokofa swayed before a chasm filled with countless tembo bones. Some bones were bleach white with age while others still carried the stench of death, grey flesh still attached to them. The tembo woman's chants were unintelligible to Changa, but they agitated Shangé. Her face bunched, her eyes narrowed.

"You and I will attack Nokofa," she whispered. "Yusef, you and Mijoga must work your way down to the chasm. Don't let anything emerge."

Yusef nodded, but his drooping eyes and downturned mouth expressed his misgivings. Changa had no time to reassure him; Shangé bolted over the hill and crept down toward Nokofa. Changa hurried up to her and they worked their way through the sparse foliage together.

"Remember, our goal is the talisman."

Changa could see the strip of skin encircling Nokofa's head glowing with the light of the bone pit.

"Let's end this," he said.

Changa snatched a throwing knife from his sash, took aim and hurled it at Nokofa's head.

"No, Changa!" Shangé reached for his hand too late. Nokofa spun, batting the knife away with her shoka then leaped toward them. Shangé shoved Changa aside and Nokofa landed where they stood, her blade splitting the ground. Shangé pounced, both blades flailing. Changa scrambled to his feet, sword in one hand, throwing knife in the other. He was sure Shangé's furious assault would give him an advantage. He was wrong. Nokofa slapped his blades away the swung the shoka blade at his scalp. He ducked, the blade passing inches from his head. Shangé and Changa's speed prevented Nokofa from attacking them but neither of them could penetrate her defense.

Something wrapped around Changa's waist, crushing the breath from him. He rose into the air, the pressure increasing. He looked down at the translucent appendage encircling him then up into the cold eyes of a resurrected tembo. He stabbed the nefarious limb and the tembo screeched. Changa fell, his dense body smashing into the foliage. He lay stunned, gasping for air when Yusef's face appeared above him.

"I'm sorry kibwana," he said. "There were too many of them."

A cacophony of trumpeting rose from the chasm. Nokofa managed to raise her minions despite Shangé's relentless attack. Mijoga dashed back and forth along the chasm edge, roaring, biting and slashing at the hundreds of spectral tembos emerging from the pit. Yusef ran to assist him; Changa climbed to his feet and staggered toward the fighting females. Changa's return was too late. As he ran to Shangé, Nokofa's shoka slipped by Shangé's sword and sank into her ribcage. Shangé's swords tumbled from her hands as she collapsed. Nokofa straddle her, the bloody shoka raised over her head.

"Why did you do this?" Nokofa shouted. "They condemn you and you serve them?"

Mwanamke Tembo shook her head sadly. "You always lived as a fool, Shangé. Now you shall die as one."

Changa threw his knife. The blade cut through the air with inhuman speed, aided by the concoction Shangé supplied. It struck Nokofa's head, nicking the leopard band as it knocked her off balance. Shangé screamed as she jumped to her feet, wrapped her fingers around the band and ripped it off Nokofa's wounded head. Nokofa's eyes went wide, her angry yell dying in her throat as she faded away into a luminous smoke. The shoka fell as the essence that was Nokofa ascended into the sky. The ground jolted;

Changa turned to see the tembo specters fall back into the chasm, their long dead bones animated no more by Nokofa's nyama. Yusef and Mijoga stared into the abyss for a moment, savoring their unexpected reprieve. The lion departed first, loping to Shangé. Yusef staggered to Changa.

"Is it over?" he asked.

Changa looked toward Shangé and Mijoga. "Wait."

Shangé raised her arms; her hands open to the sky. She chanted in a tongue unfamiliar to Changa's ears but her tone revealed the meaning. Brightness shifted in the sky then descended over her. Motes of light hovered then disappeared. Shangé fell to her knees, cradling her face in her palms.

Changa approached Shangé, placing his hand lightly on her shoulder. Shangé looked at him, tears trails on her soiled face.

"Go collect your tusks, Changa," she said. "Mwanamke Tembo will bother you no more."

"And what of you?" he asked.

Shangé looked away. "It seems my price is not paid yet."

It was not Changa's way to ponder about the spirits, but he was sure a wrong had been done. But there was nothing he could do. The ways of the spirits were beyond his understanding.

"Thank you, Shangé," he said. He turned to walk away.

"Wait." Changa turned to see Shangé extending Nokofa's leopard headband to him.

"Take it. It contains much nyama. It will add to yours."

"Mine?"

Shangé grinned. "You are the son of a kabaka. You were born with great nyama. You just haven't realized it yet."

Changa took the band. It seemed to vibrate in his hand for a moment then ceased. Shangé stood, holding her side. The wound, though still bleeding, was beginning to heal.

She patted Mijoga's mane and together they disappeared into the woods.

Yusef walked up to Changa. "Now is it over?"

"For us it is," Changa said. "Shangé's quest continues."

A roar echoed in the darkness and the stars above seemed to shift in response.

"Come Yusef. It's time to go home." They walked together towards the peaks, a wealth of ivory waiting for them to claim. The darkness made it difficult going but they made it to camp by daybreak. The men looked grateful and relieved, especially Nafasi. He ran to Changa, grabbing his hand and shaking it furiously.

"Allah has spared you!" he shouted.

Kenda appeared. She ignored Changa, her joyful eyes locking on Yusef's battered bulk. She ran to him, brushing by Changa to stand before his friend.

"You have come back," she said, a tinge of relief in her voice.

Changa could not remember when Yusef had smiled so without a gourd of palm wine.

"Mwanamke Tembo will harass us no longer," Changa announced. "Tomorrow we will go to the hunters' camp and gather the tusks."

Nafasi looked concerned. "Bwana, there is much ivory, more than we can carry."

"Yusef, you and Kenda will go to the village and hire more porters," Changa said. "We will prepare the tusks while you are away."

Kenda struggled to hide her smile, but Yusef 's emotions were obvious.

"Yes, we will do so!" he exclaimed.

The men built huts for Changa and Yusef, although their energy for Yusef was wasted. No sooner had night fallen did Yusef steal into Kenda's hut. The sounds seeping through the woven branches left no doubt of their feeling for each other. Changa sat alone before the fire, rolling Nokofa's headband with his fingers. Another object to add to his mysterious collection, each one said to possess some power which added to his own. Changa smirked; this so-called nyama had not helped him so far. It did not help him prevent his father execution, nor did it help him avoid years of slavery. Still, there was something about each talisman that made them worth keeping. Each one represented a significant moment in his life. One day, when he was home again, he would tell his children the story that brought the object to his hands. That day was still far away. For now, his concern was getting his tusks to Mombasa. He lay before the fire, falling into a hopeful sleep.

Before The Safari

MBOGO RETURNS

Changa Diop gazed into Mogadishu harbor from his dhow, a tangle of emotions straining his sepia bearded face. He stood at the bow, his thick arms folded across his wide chest. The azure sky displayed a smattering of clouds drifting inland with the monsoon winds. Memories emerged in his mind, images of a past that couldn't be forgotten. The beaches were busy as always, crowded with dhows from every Swahili city and many Arab cities as well. Hundreds of loincloth wearing laborers churned the normally clear water into a sandy slush as they met the boats to unload their cargo. Coral stone warehouses peered down on the familiar scene, one that was repeated in every Swahili city speckling the East African coast from the Horn to the Zambezi. Mogadishu was the northernmost of these cities, blessed with monsoon winds strong enough to push and pull ships directly to Arabia, India and beyond. Any successful merchant of the lower coast had to pass his merchandise to the Arab and Hindu traders waiting in Mogadishu to ferry the wealth of East Africa to the rest of the world.

Changa had not wished to come here, but business forced his hand. Belay, his mentor and employer, had died, leaving his merchant fleet to Changa. After rebuffing a bitter challenge by Belay's wayward sons, the young BaKonga set out to confirm the relationships Belay had established and maintained for decades. It would not be easy; the Swahili were a closed group. Their unity depended on a complex network of bloodline and relations forged through centuries of assimilation and marriage then legitimized by a strict hierarchy separating them from those they served and those who served them. To the Swahili he was a mhadimu, a freed slave, a label that identified him as someone lesser than others despite being free. To his own people, he was a prince.

His uncertainty increased as his dhow was met by Bwana Kabili's men. They nodded and pushed past him to confer with his crew and unload the stacks of ivory and tortoise shells filling the dhows broad hull. Changa held up his robes and waded ashore. He was greeted by two familiar faces, servants who would accompany him into the city. Tayari and Kazi shared weak smiles and shifted about as he approached. Tayari, a slim man with deep set eyes, bowed to him. Kazi did not.

"Welcome, Changa, I mean, bwana Diop," Tayari said. Kazi said nothing, his disapproving eyes speaking for him. Their opinion meant little to Changa, but he wondered if the attitude was a glimpse of what he would experience at Kabili's house. If so it was a wasted trip and a serious setback to his business. The men took his belongings and they set out for Kabili's home.

The three did not speak as they traveled Mogadishu's narrow crowded streets working their way around busy merchants and loaded donkeys. They eventually reached the central district, home of Mogadishu's wealthiest merchants. Kabili's house was one of the largest in the district a direct reflection of his close relation to the sultan. His courtyard gate consisted of a high coral stone archway filled with an elaborately carved ebony wood door. The servants opened the gate and beckoned Changa to follow. The courtyard was small, pots stuffed with flowers lining the walls leading to the entrance to the home. The building stood three stories high, another sign of Kabili's wealth. With Belay he had taken little notice of it; on his own the structure seemed intimidating.

"Wait here," Tayari said. "We will tell our master you have arrived." The servants disappeared into the darkness of the entrance hallway. Kabili emerged moments later, a smile on his bearded face and his arms outstretched.

"Welcome Changa! Allah has blessed you with a pleasant journey, I see."

The men embraced, striking each other hard on the back. It was as friendly a greeting a Swahili could give another. Changa relaxed. He had passed the first test.

"It is good to see you, bwana Kabili," Changa said.

"Just Kabili," the merchant replied. "You are a merchant and a friend now, Changa. There is no formality between us. Come, let us go inside."

Changa's confidence grew as he followed Kabili into his home. He had passed the second test. A small table rested before the staircase leading to the second floor, the section of the house reserved for the family, friends and trading partners. They sat and the servants served them cool water.

"I was so sorry to hear of brother Belay," Kabili said. "Every man's time must come. I'm sure he sits at the feet of Allah."

Changa nodded in agreement. He was not a Muslim, but he respected Belay's faith.

"There has been sadness and joy for his family and friends."

"Anger, too, I suspect."

Kabili was referring to Belay's sons. They had expected to inherit their father's business despite their total lack of interest and Belay's obvious disapproval of them all.

"Yes, I believe anger would be the right word," Changa agreed. "But the law is the law. Anything else was beyond their abilities."

Kabili laughed. "Your sword arm has prevented many disagreements, I'm sure."

The merchant took a sip from his cup then set it down with a finality that signaled it was time to discuss serious matters.

"What have you brought me?"

"I bring ivory and tortoise shells. I also have a small amount of iron from Sofala."

Kabili's eyebrow rose as he pursed his lips. "Iron from Benematapa? This is very interesting. The Calicut merchants will be very interested in that. Of course, they are a small matter. Abdul Saheed is the man we must please and he always has a taste for ivory. As a matter of fact, his ship arrived two days ago. I told him you would be here today and you did not disappoint."

"Where will we meet him?" Changa asked.

Kabili's face took on a nervous frame. "We will meet him tonight…at the pits."

Changa's face tightened as he pushed back a wave of anger threatening to burst from his lips. He waited before answering; hoping that when he did the disgust he felt would not emerge in his tone.

"That's not a desirable place to meet," he finally replied.

"I understand how you feel, but it is where Saheed wishes to meet. Neither of us is in a position to refuse him. He is our link to the markets in Oman."

"I would not be good company in such a place. I give you my permission to negotiate with him on my behalf. With your permission I will at my dhow until you return."

Kabili frowned. "Saheed insisted that you be present. He will not meet with me alone. He wants to see the man Belay trusted with his business."

The merchant leaned towards Changa. "You are a master merchant now. You have earned this position against the odds, so do not take it lightly. I welcomed you into my home as if you were Swahili because of my respect for Belay and his love for you. Do not make me regret my actions."

Changa wanted to slam his fist against the table and tell Kabili to go to hell. The ways of the Swahili would confound a man not used to them. Changa took the time to learn them only because Belay insisted. He did not plan on conforming to them. He had his own goal in mind, but it required him to accept Belay's gift until that time he amassed enough wealth to fulfill his own dream. That day was far from near.

"Your words carry the weight of wisdom," Changa conceded. "I will accompany you."

"Excellent! You will stay in the upstairs room. You will refresh and rest then we will set out for the pits at nightfall."

Changa watched Kabili disappear into the private section of the house before climbing the stairs to the visitor bedroom. In the past he had either slept at the dhow or at an inn in the country town. Now he resided in Kabili's home, the final test passed. The modest room contained a mahogany wood bed, a small desk and room for a prayer rug. He dropped his bags on the floor and collapsed in the bed, exhausted more from the stress of acceptance than the safari. He'd taken a small step toward building the wealth he would need to return to Bakongo and fulfill a promise. There was much more to accomplish, but at least now he could see the path clearly. His only regret was that his mentor Belay's passing had made the future possible.

Changa was awakened by a gentle tug on his shirt. A young girl with a gleaming smile nodded her head slightly.

"Bwana Diop, master Kabili awaits you in the courtyard."

Changa dismissed the girl and dressed quickly, donning his best robe and turban. Kabili waited with bodyguards and porters.

"I see you needed the rest," he said. "Come, we are late."

Kabili's men met them at the gate with provisions and donkeys. Changa was offered a beast but declined, preferring to walk after the long sea voyage. They travelled the narrow streets to the outskirts of town, premature darkness instigated by the tall buildings. The streets bustled with men and women, the men enjoying the cool evening with the day's end, the women emerging into the night as was custom for Mogadishu and other Swahili cities. Changa looked about nervously, his feet treading a well-known path. There was a difference now, but the past refused to be forgotten. He followed Kabili as an equal; seven years ago, he walked the same path as a slave.

They left the confines of the stone town and quickly passed through the country town. Non-Swahilis resided in the wood and thatch homes, free men and slaves who served as traders with and protection from the people of the interior. After the county town were the gardens, cultivated tracts of land covered with citrus groves and sorghum fields. The fields diminished and for a time they entered an area of grass and trees, a natural divide between the city and their destination. Soon they were back on a more civilized path, the sounds and smells of another type of civilization rising in the distance. A gathering of camels and donkeys blocked the entrance to the stone building, the doors flanked by two shirtless guards wearing scimitars and holding torches. Their eyes narrowed as they scrutinized the party, their hands on their hilts. Kabili's servant approached the guards and signaled toward the party; the guards relaxed and opened the doors.

A rush of sounds and smells swept over them. Changa stiffened as old memories broke out their mental chains. He resisted the excitement flowing into his skin and held back the mental ritual he learned long ago to prepare. The sounds increased as they traversed the corridor. Changa was so occupied battling his basic urges that the sudden light of the pit room startled him. He jerked up his head to the chaos of the pit area. It was a circular room lit by torches tilting from the coral walls at regular intervals. The smoke rose into the star-studded sky through the wide opening overhead. Groups of merchants and their servants surrounded the pit edge, each cluster a celebration unto itself. Servant girls danced the rim, their voluptuous bodies exposed through sheer silk pants, naked midriffs and thin veils. The smell of blood and death was pervasive.

"There he is," Kabili said, breaking Changa's sullen trance.

Abdul Saheed sat in the center of the largest group, his large frame supported by a pile of pillows. Eight armed men formed a perimeter around him as dancing girls swirled and swayed before him. A jewel goblet occupied his right hand, wine sloshing over the gilded rim as he waved his hand back and forth to the rhythm of the dancers' hips.

"Brother Saheed!" Kabili called out. Saheed pulled his eyes from the dancers and aimed them at Kabili. His frown quickly transformed into an inebriated smile.

"Ah! Brother Kabili. Come, come! I'm afraid we started the celebration without you."

Changa and Kabili made their way to Saheed's entourage. Saheed wrapped his thick arms around Kabili, squeezing him so tight Kabili grunted. The Omani looked over Kabili's shoulder into Changa's distracted eyes. Changa peered into the pit. The dirt was bloodied, the remnants of a recent fight. Two furrows bordered by boot prints meant someone was dragged away either unconscious or dead. The trial ended at stout metal door, an opening Changa had passed through many times.

"Who is this?" Changa turned his attention back to his companions.

"This is Changa Diop. He handles my business from Mombasa now."

Saheed shoved Kabili aside and staggered to Changa. He dropped his wide hands on Changa's shoulders and the BaKonga did not move. Though the Omani filled his vision, a portion of his attention stayed on the pit.

"You're not Swahili," Saheed slurred. "You're too solid a man to be a merchant. A former mercenary, perhaps?

Changa managed a polite grin. "Something like that."

Saheed made a dismissive gesture with his hand. "No matter; as long as you continue delivering that wonderful ivory of yours you have my business."

"Thank you, bwana Saheed. You have made me very happy."

Another man emerged from behind Saheed, a man whose presence sent Changa into internal rage. His turbaned head emerged over Saheed's shoulder, his thin frame swallowed by silk robes. His narrow brown face was carved in half by a golden smile matching the crown of rings embracing each finger and bracelets punctuating his arms and hands. His name was Rach. He had once served Maulani, the gruff Swahili who owned the pits, and the same man who once owned Changa. Rach had apparently assumed ownership of the pit; how and when he accomplished it Changa did not know or care. Staring into the face of a man he so despised was becoming more than he could handle. The pit owner looked into Changa's eyes and a glimmer of recognition surfaced. He opened his mouth but did not speak.

"What is it, Rach?" Saheed said impatiently.

"Bwana, the main fight is about to begin. It would be a generous gesture to my other patrons if you were to take your seat so that all could see."

Saheed chuckled. "Come, my friends. We shall drink while the champions battle for our entertainment."

Changa pushed by Rach roughly. The man's eyes followed him, but Changa realized the pit master did not recognize him, at least not yet. The three of them sat on the pillows as the crowd babbled, wagers beginning before the combatants emerged. The metal door opposite them creaked open and the crowd cheered. Two guards armed with metal orinkas emerge. The man behind them shuffled in, his legs shackled at the ankles. He wore a loincloth and a blue turban that covered his face as well as his head. The man was tall and athletically built but seemed too small for the brutal business of the pit.

"Who is this?" Kabili asked.

"They call him the Tuareg," Rach replied. "Don't let his size fool you. He is much better that he looks. He is undefeated."

"You lie," Saheed challenged. "I have seen men his size broken in half in pit fights."

"That is true, bwana, if a man could get his hands on him," Rach replied. "The Tuareg moves like a dancer and strikes like a mamba. You will see."

The guards unshackled the Tuareg and backed away from him to the door. The dungeon door was opened and three fighters entered. They were bare-chested as well, varying from dark brown skin to pale white. Each man was heavily muscled, strength developed in the confines of pit stone. Each also held a dagger.

"Why are they armed?" Changa asked.

Rach looked at him a moment before answering. Changa could tell the man was trying to remember him. The pit master shook his head then smirked.

"You will see."

The three dagger men move cautiously but the Tuareg did not. He sprang at the closest man then ducked as the man thrust his dagger. The Tuareg swept his feet away, taking the man's dagger before he struck the sand. He was attacking the two others as the third lay sprawled bleeding at the neck. Changa's eyes went wide as the other gasped; he never saw the Tuareg slit the man's throat. Like Rach described, the fighter danced between the two fighters, striking with knife, feet and fists. Minutes later the other two men lay in the sand with their cohort.

"He's amazing!" Saheed exclaimed.

"He truly is," Rach said. "I haven't seen anyone better since…since Mbogo!"

Rach's head jerked towards Changa. His eyes were wide, fear wrinkling his forehead as his hands shook. Changa smiled.

The pit door opened again and more fighters flooded the pit. Some were armed, others were bare handed. It was a score at least. The Tuareg shuffled backwards and pressed his back against the wall.

"What is this?" Kabili asked. His face was not pleasant.

"This is a free-for-all," Rach replied. "Except in this case, it is all against the Tuareg."

"He won't survive," Saheed said. "What in Shaitan's name are we betting on?"

"We bet on how long he lives," Rach answered with a golden smile.

Changa's reaction was reflexive. He smashed his fist into Rach's mouth, knocking free a number of his gold teeth. He then took off his turban and shirt, dropping them at Kabili's feet.

"Changa, no!" Kabili warned.

But Changa did not hear him. He heard the chattering of the betters and the clattering of their coin on the betting trays. He saw the fighters edging closer to the Tuareg, no man eager to be the first one to reach him. He watched the Tuareg press himself against the wall, his eyes moving from left to right. He would not let this happen.

Changa leaped into the pit. He landed on three fighters opposite the Tuareg, injuring all three with his bulk. A fighter turned to look at him and Changa kicked the man in the gut then hammered his fist on the back of the man's head. Other fighters turned toward him and Changa attacked. Then he heard it, a chorus that had not touched his ears for years, and a chant that angered and energized him simultaneously.

"Mbogo... Mbogo... Mbogo!

Changa could not claim the grace of the Tuareg, but he more than made up for it with his power, speed and experience. Fighter crumbled before his murderous barrage, his limbs fueled by the injustice of the situation and the rhythmic chant of his name. Changa fought until his fists swung at air. His heavy arms fell to his side; his chest heaving. The crowd roared even louder. Changa looked about, waiting for more men to spill from the door. Instead, he saw the Tuareg standing before him, surrounded by a pile of broken and moaning men. Changa knew then what the revelers wanted.

He stepped over an unconscious fighter and approached the Tuareg. The man with the hidden face stood still, his arms folded before his chest. Changa stopped a safe distance away and extended his hand. The Tuareg's eyes gleamed and he grasped Changa's hand. Together they raised their hands and the crowd cheered. Coins rained down on them.

"No!" Rach stood at the edge of the pit, blood running from his wounded mouth. The pit guards surged around him, pushing Kabili, Saheed and his entourage against the wall. The spectators mumbled, confused stares passing back and forth.

"This is my pit!" Rach growled. "If I sentence a man to death, then he dies. No one challenges my authority, not even you, Mbogo!"

An evil smile came to the pit master's face. "Free all the fighters! I offer a pouch of gold and a woman for the man that kills the Tuareg… and Mbogo!"

The pit door burst open once more, the lower guards rushing away from the coming onslaught of dozens of fighters. But they were not the first to reach the duo. Spectators jumped into the pit with swords, clubs, and chairs. Rach's offer was too enticing to pass up, even for those who pretended to possess wealth. Changa and the Tuareg instinctively stood back to back against the torrent of greedy assailants. Changa closed his eyes for a moment, seeking that calm place in his mind which prepared him for the carnage he was about to deliver. He released his fury on the first man that reached him, a young bearded Swahili servant brandishing a battered iron sword. He slapped the sword aside and grasped the man by the neck and the waist then lifted him over his head. With a yell that startled his attackers he threw the man into the mass, tearing the blade from his hands as he disappeared into the mass. Bodies fell before him and were trampled by the others hoping to claim the rich prize. Changa met their greed with desperate fury, cutting wide swaths with the sword. Dead and wounded men collapsed before him with each swing of his powerful arms. The mob pressed closer to him but Changa's strength did not waver. He tapped a well of fury filled by his past, rage created the day his father was slain before him by the sorcerer who stole his father's throne and chased an eight-year-old heir in to slavery. He did not know of the Tuareg's condition nor did he care, for in his state every man bore the face of Usenge and every man had to die.

The avaricious human tide subsided. Those that did not lay dead or dying in the sand were scrambling to the wall, climbing away from the death dealers of the pit. But there was no respite; the true fighters had reached the pit. Death did not dampen Rach's offer to the dungeon dwellers. To them, death would be their eventual companion no matter what the outcome. Gold to buy better food and a woman to ease their bondage was worth challenging the dangerous warriors before them.

The Tuareg stood beside Changa. Changa glanced at the man as he wrapped his bloodied hands with rags from his unfortunate attackers. He gave Changa a serious look and together they charged into the fighters. Changa settled into his instinctive rage, blade and fists meeting the practiced determination of the pit fighters. He struck and was struck back; he fell and climbed back to his feet, jumping back into the melee. Above the din of conflict, he heard the chanting of his name, the raw rhythm filling his passion. Like the first wave the second attack subsided then ceased. Changa fell to his knees, gasping for breath. He managed to lift his head and saw the Tuareg sitting with his legs drawn up, his head hanging between his knees. The turbaned warrior lifted his head to look at Changa, his eyes filled with victorious gratitude.

A foul awareness entered Changa's mind and he closed his eyes in response. The sensation seeped like a rank scent from the bowels of the dungeon, its intensity increasing with each passing moment. Changa turned away from the Tuareg, his face resigned to what was about to occur. The sound of calloused skin sliding against stone accompanied the foreboding creeping up his back and into his battered limbs.

The true reason Changa feared Mogadishu emerged into the pit. To the crowd it appeared as a huge man ducking through the dungeon portal, his umber skin barely containing the muscles writhing with each motion. To Changa it appeared in its true form, a hulking mass of ashen skin. Small red eyes peered at him, its tusk filled mouth turned up at the corners into a distorted smile. The pit fell silent. The tebo had found him again.

The Tuareg attempted to stand but Changa waved him back down.

"You cannot help with this one," Changa said. "It has come for me. Only I can deal with it."

The tebo lumbered closer to him, its stench heavy on its breath.

"You were foolish to return here, son of Mfumu," it grunted. "Usenge's curse still stands."

"I will run from you no longer," Changa replied. "As you can see, I am no longer a boy."

The tebo's laugh resembled the gurgling of a drowning man. "It does not matter. Death has no preference."

The tebo's arm flashed at Changa. The blow caught his shoulder, knocking him into the air and against the stone wall. Changa laid stunned, bright flashes hovering about his head. The lights dissipated as the tebo appeared into his view from above, his bulk plunging down at Changa.

Changa rolled and the ground beside him shook. He staggered to his feet and stumbled to the wall below Kabili and Saheed.

"Throw me my robe!" he shouted. Kabili tossed Changa's robe into the pit. Changa jumped up, grabbing the garment as it floated down. The tebo was charging, moving faster that a creature its size should. But there was nothing natural about the tebo. It was a captured soul of a dying nganga sent to do Usenge's bidding. Changa searched the folds of his robe for the throwing knife he'd hidden inside, the only object that could stop the spirit. He yanked the talisman free and the tebo stopped, its red eyes blinking.

"Your trinket will not save you," it said.

"We shall see," Changa spat back.

The tebo bellowed and rushed Changa again. Changa sidestepped the creature then grabbed his arm. He was disgusted as his hand sank into the tebo's dead flesh. He swung himself onto the tebo's back, pressing the knife into its thick neck leaned back, tightening his grip with all his weight and might. The tebo scrambled backwards, slamming Changa into the wall but the BaKonga would not let go. It repeated the move again and again, each time stunning Changa with waves of pain. But he would not loosen his grip. He had run from Usenge and his minions all his life. He would run no longer.

The tebo fell to one knee and grasped at the enchanted iron cutting its neck. Changa pulled tighter, his teeth clinched, his hands bleeding as the small shells cut into his skin. Suddenly the tebo shuddered and let out a piercing wail. Its flesh gave way and the knife sliced through its neck. Changa fell backwards as the creature fell forward and crashed into the sand, putrid ooze pouring from its headless body.

Changa was barely conscious when more commotion reached his ears.

"No, no, put me down! Put me down!"

Changa looked up to the seating area. Saheed's guard shuffled to the edge of the pit holding squirming Rach over their heads. The remnants of the throng, those who were prudent enough not to jump into the pit, began to clap and chant.

"Throw…him! Throw…him!

The guards looked to Saheed. The Omani was clearly sober and furious. He snapped his head up and down and the guards threw Rach into the pit.

Changa managed to stand. He picked up his robe and made his way to the cowering pit master.

"Mbogo please, do not kill me!" Rach begged. "Anything you ask is yours!'

Changa reached into his robe and extracted a small bag of gold.

"The Tuareg is mine," he said.

Changa kicked Rach in the face. The man sprawled onto his back unconscious. Changa placed the gold on his chest. He walked stiffly back to the Tuareg and lifted the man to his feet. The spectators cheered; Saheed gazed at him with admiration; Kabili shook his head and smiled. The pit guards came to them warily, their hands raised in submission.

"What do you wish, Mbogo?" the taller one asked.

"This man belongs to me now. Give him clothing and set him free."

The guards bowed and led the Tuareg back into the lower pit.

Changa climbed out of the pit and returned to his companions. Saheed reached out and grabbed his bruised shoulder. Changa winced.

"You are magnificent!" he exclaimed. "Belay was truly a blessed man. I am proud to have you as a trading partner. I will double my orders from you. Double!"

"Thank you, bwana," Changa fell before them, the furious battles finally taking their toll. Kabili was the first to his side.

"You will stay with me until you recover," he whispered. "I had hoped your presence would help sway Saheed to a better deal. This was not the way I had planned."

Changa spent weeks recovering under Kabili's care. Saheed paid all the expenses, sending the best physicians and healers to tend his wounds. The streets of Mogadishu buzzed with the story of Mbogo's return, spurring even more interest in Kabili's business.

Twenty days after arriving in Mogadishu Changa finally returned to his dhow. He was a richer man that when he arrived and he was much more content. The tebo was dead which meant he was free of Usenge's nyama, for how long he did not know. His baharia greeted him enthusiastically, each man proud to serve the master of the pits. They seem to have anticipated his intentions for the ship was waiting to sail. Someone else waited to greet him, a man draped in blue robes, a sword hanging from his shoulder in a leather baldric. The man's face was covered as it had been in the pit.

Changa extended his hand. "You are a slave no more. You are free to go wherever you wish or you can accompany us to Mombasa. I could use a man with your skills."

The Tuareg nodded, placing his hand on his chest. He then gestured toward the dhow.

Changa was puzzled. "You cannot speak?"

The Tuareg shook his head then placed a finger where his lips were hidden beneath his veil.

"A vow of silence?"

The Tuareg nodded. Changa frowned. This was a situation he didn't anticipate.

"This could make things difficult." Changa looked over the Tuareg's shoulder to the dhow. It was ready.

"Come, my friend. It's time we left this place. I suspect neither one of us will visit any time soon."

The two marched through the sand to the waiting dhow. Changa took a last glance at the city. His business was secure and a part of him was content. He would never see Mogadishu again.

WALAJI DAMU
(THE BLOOD EATERS)

Shangé crouched on the balls of her feet, her swords drawn. She stared into the thick brush before her, waiting for the sounds rushing toward her to make known their source. Whatever the creature was revealed to be, she knew why it was running her way. Mijoga had been hunting most of the morning and his persistence finally bore fruit. Fruit what kind, she did not know.

The bushes jolted leaves flung in every direction. The ground vibrated against her soles; whatever was coming her way was large. Mijoga's familiar roar was answered by a husky bellow and Shangé's eyes widened. Mijoga was driving a buffalo toward her. She lost her rhythm as the beast rumbled side to side, dodging trees like a dancer and trampling shrubs like a tembo. Its eye rolled with fear and pain then focused on her. A black mane rose above the foliage, a familiar roar bouncing off the trees. Mijoga had done his part, now it was her turn.

Shangé remained in the path of the charging bull, moving her lips and she silently counted. The bull was before her, its head lowered its horns inches from her chest. Shangé jumped then twisted, landing on the bulls back facing in his direction. She lay flat its back and reached down with both blades. In one motion she cut the bull's throat then somersaulted off its back and landing on her feet. The bull crashed into a thick tree and tumbled sideways into the brush. It shook for a moment then lay still.

Shangé sheathed her swords and approached the bull. An agitated roar stopped her; she turned to see Mijoga stalking toward her, his ears flat on his head, his tail jerking threateningly.

"No, Mijoga," she pleaded. "Do not go. Do not leave me."

Her fears were coming true. Mijoga, the spirit of her mortal lover, was losing his struggle against the spirit of the simba he possessed. The creature approaching her did not see his fallen companion; it only saw an object between it and its prey.

Shangé stared into Mijoga eyes and extended her ka inside him. Mijoga shook his head and roared, attempting to clear her from his mind. She reached deep, searching for the glow she knew as Mijoga the warrior. She found it pulsing weakly, fading into the darkness of the simba's mind. She shared her ka touching his waning spirit with hers. The union of both spirits was orgasmic and exhausting. Shangé knew what she did was dangerous to her, for every contact with Mijoga drained her ka as well. She had already lost the strength to return to the heavens. If she continued she would lose her ability to serve.

Mijoga's ka was renewed. She withdrew her ka, blinked and found herself staring into the simba's complacent face, and his snout inches from hers. He rumbled and licked her cheek with his rough tongue. Shangé grasped handfuls of his mane and shook his head from side to side.

"Stay with me, Mijoga," she whispered. "We'll be free soon."

She wished she believed her words. She set about the task of butchering the buffalo. Mijoga waited with human patience and was finally rewarded with meat. Shangé's respite would take much longer. After butchering the carcass, she gathered wood and leaves, constructing a smoker to preserve the meat. Toward nightfall she finally ate, enjoying the succulent flesh with wild yams and fruit. She was covered with blood and smelled of smoke. She remembered a lake nearby so she packed up the smoked meat and carried it to the lake shore. She stripped off her clothes and bathed, the warm water soothing her wounds. She washed out her clothes, hung them to dry then laid out her blanket on the soft grass. Her eyes searched the heavens, worry heavy on her mind. It had been weeks since she heard from the spirits. Ever since she fell from their presence and receive their sentence they had demanded her service. But lately that demand had waned and it concerned her. She had certainly not done enough to earn their forgiveness for she was still mortal and Mijoga was still a simba. A fearful thought came to her; had they abandoned her? If so, there was no hope for the two of them. Mijoga would eventually succumb to the nature of the simba and she would be alone. There were others that could help her but they required a price she wasn't willing to pay.

Go to the Land of Lakes," the voice in her head spoke. The command came so suddenly Shangé jerked upright and awoke Mijoga.

"The people suffer from an old foe," the voice continued.

"Who is it?" Shangé asked. There was no response.

Shangé wasted no time. She packed up her belongings and supplies then dressed.

"Come, Mijoga. Maybe this time we will be rewarded."

*   *   *

The Land of the Lakes ran along a rugged valley sliced into the surrounding hills by a jagged celestial knife. The lakes sprawled among green mountains, huge bodies of water that held abundant fish and attracted large numbers of animals. The rivers that accompanied the lakes were violent entities, their swift waters often torn by large stretches of cataracts that could smash the sturdiest canoes into splinters. The people of the land paid homage to both lakes and rivers; praising the lakes for their sustenance and fearing the rivers for their power.

Shangé emerged from her hut overlooking a wide river snaking between two huge lakes. For weeks she and Mijoga waited for the next instructions from the spirits but none had come. She walked to the hill slope, casting her restless eyes on the river below. Though signs of human life abounded, she had seen no one. She was beginning to wonder about the wisdom of the spirits when Mijoga appeared over the slopes, his actions speaking for him.

"Someone is coming," she said aloud. She went to the opposite side of hill. A procession of people emerged from the forest. They wore simple clothing made from bark, their bodies covered by white chalk patterns. Two of the people, young bare-chested men with bird tattoos on their stomachs, carried a large bronze statute resting on a wooden platform. An old man led them, his body covered by a cotton robe that brushed his bare feet. They chanted a song as they struggled up the hill, a song Shangé was well familiar with. It was a plea for the spirits help.

Shangé waited as they climbed. Her impatience gave way to sympathy as the villagers came into view. These were poor, fearful people. The statue they bore was probably an accumulation of their wealth transformed to an offering to insure the spirits intervention. It was also a waste; whatever these people wanted would not be bought by any material offering.

Shangé was sitting when the pilgrimage reached her. The people stood back, their trepidation apparent in their averted eyes. The priest seemed just as afraid, his head trembling as the bearers place down the idol.

"Great priestess," the priest announced with a quaking voice. "We have come to pay you homage as you requested. Please accept this idol as a symbol of our gratitude."

As Shangé stood to inspect the idol Mijoga emerged from behind the hut. The people cried in terror and fled down the hill.

"No!" the priest shouted, his voice surprisingly strong for an old man. Mijoga felt the nyama in his command and smiled. The priest was stronger than he looked.

Mijoga jogged to her side and she rubbed his head.

"Do not be afraid," she said. "He is my companion."

The people returned to the positions, prostrating before her.

"Tell me what troubles you," Shangé said

"Three moons ago the ground shook," the priest began. This is not unusual for our land for we are close to the gods and often feel their restlessness. What happened days later is what gave us fear. Our people began to disappear during the night, one by one. We would find them dead days later, the blood gone from them. We have called on you for weeks once we realized our gris-gris would not protect us. The people will not leave their huts. Crops die in the fields and the animals go unfed. No one has seen whatever it is that has caused this terror to us. The people call it walaji damu, blood eater."

Shangé did well to hide her puzzlement. She had lived countless years among the spirits and witnessed many strange and wonderful things among men. Never had she seen anything like the priest described.

"What is your name, grandfather?" she asked.

"Majambere."

"Take me to your village, Majambere. We will discover the cause of this."

Majambere's village was a modest gathering of homes crowded by the banks of a small lake. They were fishermen and farmers, their only livestock a small herd of goats. The villagers that had not come to the hill were hurrying to complete their chores, their eyes constantly darting to the darkening horizon.

"It is almost time," Majambere said. "The walaji damu will come tonight."

"How are you so sure?" Shangé asked.

"The moon will not shine tonight. They always come when it's darkest. That is why we came for you today."

Majambere's followers scattered as soon as they reached the marketplace.

"Hurry!" he urged. "Finish your tasks and get into your homes!"

"What will happen now?" Shangé questioned.

"They will go inside and lock their doors." The priest face took on a dim cast. "I will hang gris-gris over their doors and chant for the spirits to protect us through the night."

Shangé knew the answer to her question before she asked. "Does it help?"

"For some," he confessed. "The walaji damu do not fear our gods."

Shangé patted Mijoga's head. "They will learn different tonight."

She pointed toward the huts. "Go among the huts. I'll stay here in the market. If this thing appears among the huts drive it to me. Hopefully it will choose an easier target."

Mijoga rumbled and trotted to the huts. The priest was still standing beside her, his eyes following Mijoga.

"He understands you?"

"He is not what he seems," Shangé said. "Go home, Majambere. We will handle this."

The priest bowed and scurried away. Shangé watched him until he was in his home then sat cross-legged in the center of the marketplace. She took out her swords and lay them before her then closed her eyes, extending her senses over the surrounding area.

A deep darkness descended on the village. Shangé kept her eyes closed, using her acute senses to track those moving through the night. The unusual quiet was a sign of strange things. Shangé sensed no movement other that herself and Mijoga, who paced restlessly among the huts. The prayers of the villagers drifted to her ears, the same prayers that once rose to her when she was among the spirits.

A celestial warning shattered her concentration and her eyes snapped open. An object dropped from above, hurtling toward her. Shangé grabbed her swords and jumped to her feet as the object landed before her. It was a being unlike any she encountered. Its skin was grey like ash, its wide head mounted on a short thick neck. It was blind, but its large ears and wide nose reveal it had evolved to its state. It held a crude spear with an obsidian point in its gnarled hand. Its mouth opened and a piercing sound cut into Shangé's ears. She stumbled away from the creature, its spear barely missing her throat. She threw up a sword instinctively, knocking the spear away. The other sword swing was planned. It sliced the creature's abdomen and it shrieked again before crumbling into its own guts.

Two more creatures landed before her, shrieking and thrusting their spears. Shangé blocked and dodged, amazed at their speed and strength. More creatures landed in the village, running to the huts. They were met by Mijoga, the simba charging from the darkness and unperturbed by their sharp screams. Some of them broke away and flailed at the huts but Majambere's magic held firm, at least for the moment. Shangé cut a creature's arm off then sliced the other at the knee, crippling it. She sprinted to help Mijoga just as the door to one of the huts succumbed to the creatures' onslaught. The walaji damu unleashed their shrieks on the hapless villagers, rendering them unconscious. Shangé watched horrified as the creatures lifted the villagers easily onto their shoulders then jumped into the darkness. The other creatures fled as well, jumping after their companions.

Majambere burst from his hut. He ran to Shangé, eyes wide and watering.

"There have never been so many! They came to take us all!"

The others emerged, falling to their knees and lifting their hands to the spirits. Then they saw the violated hut. A wail rose from the village, a lament of pain and loss.

"I failed you," Shangé said.

"No, priestess, you did not," Majambere said. "If you were not here our village would be no more."

Shangé dropped her head. The dead creature lay between her and Majambere. The others she wounded were gone. It was then she noticed their blood. The thick liquid glowed, giving off a faint bluish light. Shangé smiled.

"I will bring your people back," she said.

"I will go with you," Majambere answered. "I may be able to help."

"No. Stay with your people. They will need your strength and your protection. "Mijoga!"

The simba loped to her. Shangé pointed at the blood and Mijoga roared confidently. Together they ran into the night, following the creatures' luminous spoor.

The trail led them to a jagged rip in earth, a crevice crowded with fallen trees and animal carcasses. Shangé had seen the results of earthquakes before; it was how the Land of The Lakes was formed. Another thought began to creep into her head and the reason for her being here became clear. Just as there were spirits in the sky, there were spirits in the earth. And like the spirits in the sky, some were not passive observers.

Mijoga paced. Though he had no knowledge of Shangé's premonition it was obvious he sensed something more than a pursuit of some strange man forms. Shangé stroked his mane as she refocused on her immediate task to save the villagers.

"There,' she said. A speck of walaji damu blood glistened on the edge of the crevice. They continued the pursuit, clambering into the darkness of the tear. For hours they moved among debris from the surface, but as they traveled deeper the surroundings transformed into gray stone and stagnant cold. The darkness dispersed, replaced by a weak luminance resembling the walaji damu's blood. The weird light made the trail harder to see, but Shangé's sight eventually adjusted. They were entering another world, a world that existed beyond the touch of Jua and the power of the spirits. The light emitted from everything; the rocks, the stalactites and stalagmites, dousing them with a greenish hue. Glowing insects crawled about the ground and the walls, giving the caverns a sense of movement that unnerved her. They walked through the strange region for hours until the lighted beings dimmed into darkness. Shangé hesitated before entering, waiting for her eyes to adjust. Even with her heightened vision it was still difficult to see ahead. Mijoga expressed his discomfort with a snort and a shake of his head. The walaji damu spoor glowed even brighter, a morbid beacon to its source.

The dark caverns told a different tale that the luminous world. The walls were smooth, the ground rough yet passable. This was no random cave formed by the whims of the spirits; this was a cavern built by skilled hands.

Mijoga roared and shook his head. Shangé looked puzzled until she heard it, a thin piercing sound growing from the back of her mind. Mijoga roared again then fled back the way they came.

"Mijoga! Wait!" she shouted. The sound increased; Shangé covered her ears to stop the mysterious shriek but it increased with every moment. She fell to her knees, screaming hysterically as if her own voice could drown out the sound that stabbed her head like a hot assegai. A deeper darkness settled about her; she was losing consciousness. Something cold gripped her shoulders and a sharp sudden brightness cleared her head for a brief moment. She saw a pale, fanged face then passed out.

* * *

Shangé awoke in pain. The strange emission was gone, replaced by a lingering hum that weighed on her senses. She tried to move; something heavy pressed down on her shoulders, pinning her against a hard surface that pricked her chest. Another deeper pain surfaced on the side of her neck, a dull throb pulsing with the rhythm of her heart.

Images writhed before her. Her eyes slowly responded to the dull light around it and the images gained details.

Walaji damu danced before a glowing pile of luminous rock, each creature holding a crude stone cup in their hands. Another creature stood atop the pile draped in an indigo robe sparkling with clear stones reflecting the strange light. The creature swayed with the simple cadence in time with the others waving a thick staff over its head.

Shangé twisted her head about. The stolen villagers lay trapped to her right. They knelt before a stone dais, their hands tied behind their backs. A huge stone yoke pressed them down onto the dais. A hollow tube protruded from their necks. Blood dripped from the tube into a stone gourd propped beside the dais. Shangé surmised she was trapped the same way, her blood adding to the feast of the walaji damu.

The blood priest descended the mound and walked towards her. Shangé's strength increased with each second, her body healing rapidly. By the time the priest reached her she felt strong. She waited; there was a reason for this ceremony beyond what she observed so far. She would remain still until she discovered it.

The priest took the gourd fill with her blood. He sipped it and his eyes widened. He turned his back to her and spoke in their shrill language, his sounds similar to the sound that rendered her helpless. The others responded, their movements more vigorous. They assaulted the mound, each one grabbing a portion and raising it high over their heads. The blood priest marched past them and they followed it deeper into the cavern, the light fading fast.

Shangé gritted her teeth and clinched her fists as she pushed her hands apart. The cords binding her wrists held for a moment then snapped like dry straw. She gripped her yoke and grunted, lifting the slab of stone over her shoulders and pitching it forward. It crashed and shattered, shaking the dais on which she lay. She winched as she snatched the blood tube from her neck. Shangé felt about and found her swords propped against the dais. The walaji damu had been confident in her capture and underestimated her abilities. She secured her blades and went to free the others. The villagers had not fared as well as her. They were barely alive, each unconscious and barely breathing. Shangé was torn between trying to help them and pursuing the cave creatures until a familiar voice sealed her decision.

"I will help them." Shangé turned to see Majambere standing behind her, his face illuminated by a seeing stone dangling from his neck.

"You followed us?" she asked.

Majambere nodded. "You travelled too quickly for me to catch up to you. I found you here but there was nothing I could do. I was relieved when the walaji damu left and you freed yourself. Forgive me for my weakness."

"There is nothing to forgive," Shangé assured him. "See to your people. I must go after the walaji damu."

"Wait." Majambere reached into his pouch and extracted another seeing stone.

"You may not need this, but it will help." He looked about curiously. "Where is your simba?"

Fear crept into her head. "I don't know."

Majambere smiled weakly. "I'm sure you will find him, or he will find you."

Shangé put the seeing stone around her neck and ran in pursuit of the walaji damu. She ran as fast as the darkness allowed, hoping to close the gap between them. The darkness before her gave way to dim light; she was closing in on the procession. She slowed her pace, staying just close enough to follow. She eventually found herself in another cavern, this one more worn and ragged. Though smooth stone covered the ground, the walls showed signs of decay and stalactites dripped from the canopy. The voice of the blood priest rose over the mumbling of the walaji damu as the creatures gathered at the far end of the cavern. Shangé found an outcrop and climb it to see over the throng.

The blood priest stood before a looming grey figure. Its face resembled that of a bat, but its body was more man-like. Long fangs protruded from its long mouth, gleaming in the light. The blood priest placed the gourd of her blood before the statue then fell to his knees. The other fell as well, prostrating before the statue.

But it was no statue. Shangé gasped as a thin tongue extended from the creature's mouth and into the gourd. The tongue pulsed and grew thicker; its mouth gaped and the narrow eyes scanned slowly from side to side.

Shangé slid her swords free. This is what she was sent to do. The walaji damu were not her task, it was the monstrosity awakening before her. She eased off the out-cropping and crept toward the gathering.

The creature extended its limbs and the walaji damu began their erratic dance. The blood priest raised its gourd and staff, seeming to urge the creature upward. It stretched to its full height, its massive head breaking the stalactites overhead. The eyes blinked and recognition replaced re-pose. It struck like a viper, engulfing the blood priest.

The walaji damu froze. The creature snapped up two more before they ran, their high pitch cries no longer stun-ning Shangé. She was ready for them now, but the hapless beings fleeing around her were no longer her target. She ran towards the blood beast, her swords spread like lethal wings. The creature tossed its head back to swallow its morbid meal. She stopped before it, looking up into the harrowing visage.

The beast struck faster than she anticipated. She barely escaped its bite, stumbling away while swinging down with her sword. The blade grazed its cheek and the crea-ture screeched. It swung its head to the side, slamming it into Shangé and sending her sprawling across the stone. She rolled away from the creature's relentless surges, its head slamming against the stone, the blows having no ef-fect on its ferocity. Shangé finally rolled to her feet and sprang to her left to avoid another thrust. She ducked, the beast's claws grazing her scalp. She crossed her swords over her head, catching its wrist between the blades then slicing through flesh and bone. The claw smacked the stone and the creature screeched. It flailed, the bloody stump spewing black blood in every direction. Shangé stepped and slipped, her head thumped against the stone and she briefly blacked out. When she came to the creature was charging her again; she struggled against the throbbing pain in her skull.

The blood creature lunged. Shangé waited then rolled, avoiding the head strike and the grasping arms. She planted her feet then sprang up, both swords pointed above her head. The blades plunged into the beast's throat up to the hilts. It moaned and toppled on to its back, dragging Shangé with it. She found herself standing on its chest as it gurgled, its chest sagging inward before ceasing.

Shangé tore her swords from its throat. She scrambled off the carcass onto the bloody floor. She staggered back to the first cavern where she saw Majambere beside the dais nursing his villagers. Her head throbbed and her body ached but she was alive.

She hobbled over to the villagers.

"Can they walk?"

Majambere shook his head. "Not yet. It will take time for them to regain their strength."

"We don't have time," Shangé warned. "The walaji damu will come back. We must be gone before then."

A strident roar splintered the tense silence. Majambere and the other cowered but Shangé grinned. She knew the sound well, the triumphant call of Mijoga. He strode into their light, his muzzle, mane and claws caked with blood.

"There is no need to hurry now," she told the others. "Our way is clear."

The villagers needed only a few more hours to heal then the party set out for the surface. As Shangé said their way was clear except for the stench of the dead walaji damu littering their course. They emerged from the rift into humid darkness eased by the starlit sky. Shangé did not look up; she feared what she might see. The village came into view and the villagers pace sped in response.

"Come! Come! We are home!" Majambere shouted.

Doors burst open and the villagers poured out, the night filled with ululations of joy. Shangé and Mijoga stayed back as the villagers hugged, kissed and danced. Majambere broke away from the celebration and prostrated before the two.

"Thank you, priestess," he said. "You have saved us."

Shangé nodded. She finally dared to look into sky. There was nothing there for her, no gleaming patterns, messages to fill her head.

"Where will you go now?" Majambere asked.

"Where I am sent," Shangé replied.

Majambere studied her for a moment. "I hope you find what you seek."

He stood, bowed, and then returned to his people and their celebration.

Shangé watched him for a moment, absently stroking Mijoga's mane.

"I hope we find what we seek," she whispered. Together they walked into the night, the stars above keeping their secrets to themselves for another day.

THE GATE

Mombasa slumbered under a sliver of a moon, the eastern monsoons blowing a warm wind across the waters. The beaches were empty save the dhows, the baharia that sailed them either gone to their homes in the stone town or country town or sleeping below their decks. The stone warehouses bordering the beach landings were empty as well, all save one small warehouse near the water's edge. In a cramped room on the second floor a wax candle burned on a writing table, illuminating the space with its wavering light. A heavy-set man sat at the table, reading numbers scribbled on the yellowed pages of his journal. He turned the pages with one hand while scratching his bearded chin with the other.

Changa closed the journal then leaned back, raising his chair onto the back legs.

"Belay, you taught me many things, but not everything," he whispered.

The day Changa learned his mentor Belay had bequeath his shipping business to the young BaKonga was a joyous day. Never before had a Swahili merchant done such a thing. It was well known among the other merchants that Belay favored Changa and treated him as a son. But to deny his blood sons the business for a non-Swahili was unheard of.

Changa's joy soon became worry. Many of Belay's old business partners were not happy with his choice and refused to do business with Changa. He still retained the ivory trade, but other business disappeared. He could barely pay his men and his bills, let alone afford the basic necessities for himself. Belay's true sons circled him like scavengers, ready to pounce in and take the business if he failed. Changa was determined not to do so.

Still, he could not continue as he was doing. He needed to find new customers and he needed to find a new source of revenue. Creditors were out of the question.

Changa pulled open the desk drawer then removed a map, spreading it on the table. It was a map of the coast with each Swahili city-state marked. His eyes rested on one particular island to the south, close to the mainland city of Sofala and the Kilwa Sultanates.

"Kilwa Malikiya," Changa said. "Could you be the answer to my troubles?"

Belay had talked often of the island. The legend said it was one of the few Swahili cities ruled by a woman, her name lost in the annals of time. It was said that she was the first to trade with the Benematapa, gathering a vast treasure of gold and ivory. After the mysterious queen died her son gained control of the island. His reign lasted only ten years. The people of Kilwa Malikiya abruptly abandoned their island, founding the cities that now made up the Kilwa Sultanate. No one knew why they left, but the rumor was that they left all their possessions behind.

Changa took out his instruments, confirming the route to the island. Belay's map was the only map that revealed the location of the island. It was an heirloom passed down through his family and the last item the old merchant gave to Changa before his death.

Changa yawned. The night was finally getting to him. He would sleep, his mind finally made up. In the morning they would sail for Kilwa Malikiya.

Changa met his crews with the sunrise. The mabaharia went about their normal maintenance duties, with Yusef yelling at them every step of the way.

"Yusef!" Changa called out. "Gather the men."

Yusef waved then hurried about as fast as his large bulk would allow. Moments later the men stood before Changa, curious looks gracing their faces.

"I don't have to tell you that my business has not been well," Changa said. "Many of Belay's friends have chosen not to do business with me. Because of this I must forge new relationships. But that does not help us now. The dhows must be maintained and we all must eat."

"What must we do, Kibwana?" Yusef said. "We will starve before we leave you."

The looks on the others faces told Changa that they did not agree with his bulky friend.

"There is a place that may hold the answer to our dilemma," Changa said. "Kilwa Malikiya."

One of the baharia stepped forward, a short man as broad as he was tall.

"What's on your mind, Niko?" Changa asked.

"Every man here has heard of Kilwa Malikiya, bwana," he said. "It is not real. It is a myth."

Changa reached into his bag then took out Belay's map.

"I was given this map by Bwana Belay before he died. It is a map that shows the location of Kilwa Malikiya. I plotted a route to the island last night."

The men gathered around him, staring at the map. Niko shook his head.

"Many maps are wrong, bwana," he said. "Just because this one shows the island does not mean it exists."

Changa nodded as he rolled up the map. "I'm not asking anyone to come with me. I plan to set sail this afternoon. I would love to have my crew around me, but I will not ask you to risk your lives on a safari that may not bear fruit. Each man makes his own decision."

"They say other things about Kilwa Milikiya as well, bwana," Niko said.

"If you believe the city is a myth, why would believe anything else said about it?" Changa asked.

"I am with you kibwana!" Yusef announced.

Changa grinned. "Thank you, Yusef."

One by one the baharia joined Changa and Yusef. Soon only Niko stood opposite them.

"I can't," he said. "I will not follow a myth."

Changa approached Niko then placed a friendly hand on his shoulder.

"I understand, Niko. Go be with your family. There will be a place for you with my crew when we return."

"I hope that you do," Niko said.

Niko walked away, peering back at the others until he merged into the Mombasa crowds.

"Yusef, you will come with me to the market. We must gather supplies for the journey," Changa said.

"Yes, kibwana."

"The rest of you prepare the dhow. We set sail as soon as Yusef and I return."

Changa visited his counting room before they visited the market. He opened his chest then frowned. There was enough for supplies to take them to and from the island. If there was no treasure on Kilwa Malikiya he would be ruined.

Yusef entered the room.

"Kibwana, are you ready?" he said.

Changa closed the chest then lifted it.

"Yes, Yusef. I'm ready."

The two spent the remainder of the day procuring supplies from the market. When they returned they loaded supplies on the dhows then shared a meal with the men on the docks. Changa didn't return to his counting room that night; instead he slept on deck with his crews, savoring the open air and the clear skies. There was a time in his life long ago when his view was that of a stone room to a small cell. His days were filled with training; when he wasn't training he was fighting for his life. Since the day he fled his homeland twenty years ago his life had been one struggle after another. To lie on his back and gaze at the stars was truly a gift, a blessing he owed to Belay.

Niko's doubts intruded on his musing. The baharia was always a contrary one, but for some reason his doubts seemed to linger on Changa's mind. Changa had seen many strange and wonderful things in his life and he knew that nothing was beyond possibility. Kilwa Milikiya may be a myth, but he had to try. He had no choice.

* * *

Changa and Yusef stood at the bow of the Kazuri as it sailed into the harbor of Kilwa Milikiya. An unnatural stillness ruled the scene, the roaring waves lapping the landing beach the only sound. Sturdy docks lay empty as were the hard-packed roads leading from the shore into the stone city. No seagulls hovered overhead, the undulating fronds of palms trees the only motion. From a distance the warehouses seemed recent, but as they sailed closer the buildings revealed their neglect.

"This is not natural," Yusef said.

Changa didn't reply. He studied the shore, seeking a good place to land.

"There," he said, pointing to a stretch of beach closest to the warehouses.

The navigator steered the dhow to the landing; the baharia dropped the anchor in deeper water.

"Let's get the boats and go ashore," Changa ordered.

Yusef hesitated and Changa glared.

"We are here," he said. "We will get what we came for and we will leave. Don't let Niko's words haunt you, rafiki."

Changa and the landing crew boarded the boats and rowed to the empty beach. Once aground they headed to the nearest warehouse. The white stone was barely visible, covered by thick vines as nature reclaimed what men had abandoned. Changa hacked away the vines blocking the warehouse entrance with his machete. Stale humid air filled his nostrils as he entered the abandoned structure. The others followed, their swords at the ready.

"We'll start here," he said. "Make sure you search every corner."

For two hours they rummaged through the rotted furniture and decaying palm leaves but found nothing. They finally gave up, leaving the building, dirty, sweaty and empty handed.

Changa spotted Yusef and the other baharia coming from the warehouse opposite the docks. Yusef wiped his bald head with the palm of his hand then grimace.

"There is nothing here," Yusef said. "I think bwana Belay was wrong."

"Maybe," Changa replied. "Let's search the city. A few merchants may have left behind valuables in their homes."

Yusef sniffed. "I doubt it. Swahili are very thorough and very greedy."

"We have the time," Changa said. "We might as well."

They followed the road into the stone town. Like most Swahili cities the mosque occupied the center, and Kilwa's mosque was an impressive site despite years of neglect. The main structure rose four stories high, the crown ringed by elaborately carved ramparts. The minarets climbed even higher, their copper domes green from exposure and neglect. Changa saw movement near the top of the mosques and minarets.

"At least something lives," he said.

"Those birds are large," Yusef replied. "Vultures?"

The creatures leapt into the air simultaneously then circled the minarets, their cries echoing through the empty city.

"Those do not sound like any bird I know," Changa said. "They sound like...nyani."

"That's impossible!" Yusef said. "Nyani don't have wings!"

The flock flew toward them descending as they came closer. As their features became clear Changa's eyes went wide.

"They are nyani!" he shouted. "Run!"

The baharia sprinted for the nearest building. Changa was the first to reach the home, shoving open the door with his shoulder. He ran back into the open, waving his men to him.

"Quickly!" he shouted. "Inside!"

The men ran into the building. The flying nyani descended on the last two men, knocking them to the ground. Changa rushed to rescue them, sword in one hand, throwing knife in the other. He threw the knife; it struck one nyani in the head, knocking him off the closest man. With his sword he cleaved another nyani in two. Yusef appeared by his side, swinging his sword wildly. Together they drove the flying primates away far enough for two other baharia to grab their injured comrades and drag them into the building. Yusef and Changa stepped backwards, fending off the beasts until they were able to join their men in the building.

The primate attacked the house, tearing at the palm frond roof and beating at the doors. Changa and his men prepared themselves for the onslaught when the attack suddenly ceased, replaced by the rumble of a coming storm. Changa inched his way to the door then slowly opened it. A sky that once showed no sign of ill weather was now black with swirling clouds.

"We should not be here!" Yusef said. "This city is cursed!"

Changa looked at his friend and his men.

"Back to the dhow," he said. "We're leaving."

Changa was answered by thunder. The nyani screeched and the rumble shook the house.

Changa dared to open the door. The nyani were gone. A sudden gust of wind pushed Changa back into the house.

"It seems we're not going anywhere," Changa commented.

"We should go to the mosque," Yusef suggested. "This house will do little to protect us from the coming storm."

Changa looked incredulous. "So, you wish to go to the nyani's den?"

"Allah will protect us," Yusef said.

Thunder shook the house and rain crashed against the roof as if dumped from a well bucket. The ragged thatch ceiling gave way and the baharia were drenched.

"To the mosque!" Changa said.

The baharia splashed toward the mosque. They were almost there when an ear-piercing screech cut through the storm. Changa grimaced as he hunched and cupped his hands over his ears.

"Look!" Yusef shouted.

The dark clouds rippled above them. Changa thought he caught a glimpse of something moving through the clouds but his view was obscured by the torrential rain. The undulating clouds made a path toward their dhow. It swirled above the craft, spinning faster and faster.

"No," Changa whispered.

Bolts of lightning showered the ship, blasting the mast and deck.

"No!" Changa shouted.

Flames erupted throughout the dhow despite the rain. In moments the entire ship was engulfed in raging flames. The baharia stood stunned. Their only way home had been destroyed before their eyes. Changa's shock was brief. His mission had changed. Instead of coming to Kilwa to save his business, he had doomed it. He had to save his men and himself.

"Go," Changa said to his men. "Go!"

They ran to the mosque. Changa was the first to reach the doors, shoving them wide open. The winged nyani huddled in the center of the building. They howled at the baharia, bearing their sharp teeth. The baharia charged into the beasts, releasing their anger on them. In moment the beasts lay slaughtered. The men dragged the dead beasts from the building, tossing them into the streets. Their bodies seemed to anger the storm. It became more intense, the thunder and lightning battering the holy site. The walls and the roof of the mosque were much stronger; they held against the unnatural onslaught.

Changa slumped against the wall. Yusef sat beside him, crossing his legs.

"What will we do kibwana?" he asked.

Changa looked at his friend, his face grim.

"When the storm ceases we will go the beach and access the damage to the dhow," he said. "We'll rebuild it."

"I'm not talking about the dhow," Yusef replied. "I'm talking about this."

He waved his thick arms around.

"None of this is natural. "Flying nyani, a storm attacking our dhow; this is sorcery!"

"You are probably right," Changa said. He'd had his share of otherworldly encounters and this was very familiar. He tried to deny it, hoping the original reason for his safari would resurface, but this was no longer about finding a lost wealth. It was about survival.

There was movement at the door. Changa and the others leapt to their feet, weapons at the ready. The doors swung open and a woman entered, her wet clothing clinging to her body. She leaned against a thick carved staff, her head covered with a plain head wrap. She as she looked about Changa noticed her eyes. A milky white veil covered both orbs; the woman was blind, yet she looked about as if she could see her surroundings. She coughed, and then pulled herself straight.

"Who are you?" she asked.

Changa signaled for his men to keep their place. He approached the woman warily.

"I am Changa Diop from Mombasa," he said.

"And the others?" she asked.

"My crew," Changa replied.

"You should not be here," she said. "He will come for you soon."

"Our dhow has been destroyed," Changa said. "We won't be leaving soon. Was this your doing?"

"No," the woman replied. "He has sent his herald."

Changa looked puzzled. "His herald? Do you mean the nyani?"

The woman shook her head. "No. They are an annoyance, a side effect of his power. The inpundulu is his herald and his warning."

"We have encountered no other creature," Changa said.

"Yes, you have," the woman said. "You think this storm is natural? It's not. It is the inpundulu."

"And who are you?" Changa finally asked.

"Sayidana," she answered.

Changa lowered his sword. "Why is it that no one remains in Kilwa Milikiya except you?"

"I have not always been here," she said. "Like you I have traveled from afar."

"Where did you come from?" Changa asked.

Sayidana looked away. "Far away."

"Sofala? Pemba? Mogadishu?"

Sayidana smirked. "Much farther."

The sounds of the storm subsided.

"Listen to me, Changa. The one who claims this land is coming soon. If you and your men are here when he arrives he will kill you all. But with your help we can stop him and we all will have a chance to return home."

"So be it," Changa said. He turned to Yusef.

"When the storm clears survey the dhow and salvage what you can," Changa said. "We'll have to cut trees to repair the dhow. I'm going with Sayidana."

"That is not wise," Yusef said. "She may be the cause of our misfortunes."

Changa glanced at the woman. "I don't think so. I believe she is just as much victim as we are, but for a different reason. I plan to find out what that reason is."

Yusef's eyes said what he could not.

"If I don't return by the time the dhow is repaired, take them home," Changa said.

Changa turned to Sayidana before Yusef could reply.

"Let's go," he said.

"How many of your men are coming with us," Sayidana asked.

"Only me," Changa replied.

He grasped Sayidana's arm then lead her out the mosque. She jerked her arm away.

"I need all of you!" she said.

"You'll get only me," Changa replied. "If I take my men with us I'm sure some of them will die. I didn't bring them here for that to happen."

"The two of us cannot stop him," Sayidana insisted.

"I'm sure you haven't survived this long alone without some skills," Changa said. "And I am not easy to kill."

Sayidana's eyes seemed to glow with her sour mood. Changa braced himself for some type of attack, but the glow subsided.

"Let us go then. I hope for your sake and mine that we will be enough."

Changa nodded. "We'll have to be."

The storm waned as Changa and Sayidana made their way north from the city. It did not dissipate or travel west as most storms do. Instead it traveled the same direction Changa and Sayidana traveled.

"The inpundulu returns to its lair," Sayidana said. "It thinks it has done its duty."

"Will we see it again?" Changa asked.

"Most likely yes," Sayidana replied. "But not in this form."

They crossed from the ruined city into the surrounding forest. There was a narrow trail leading into the bush which Sayidana followed. Changa trailed close behind, his eyes studying the foliage as they passed.

"Are we going to its lair?"

"Yes. The inpundulu's lair is His citadel and his gate. We must stop him before he enters his citadel, before He can possess his full power."

"So, we will wait outside to confront him," Changa said.

"No. He will enter from within through the gate," Sayidana said.

"From inside through the gate?" Changa was confused. "How can he enter the citadel without passing through the outside? Is there a tunnel leading from the shore?"

Sayidana smiled. "You do not understand, and I'm not sure I can explain it."

Sayidana stopped by a coconut tree. A pile of coconuts lay at the base of the tree. Sayidana went to the tree then sat. She arranged the coconuts so they touched.

"What do see, Changa?"

Changa folded his arms. "I see coconuts."

"Are you sure?"

"Of course I'm sure!" Changa replied.

Sayidana grinned. "Even though these are all coconuts, they are not the same. Some are bigger, some are smaller. If we were to cut them open we would discover that some are sweeter than others, and a few may be rotten."

"What does this have to do with 'Him' and you?" Changa asked.

"The world you live in is not the only one, Changa," Sayidana said. "Like these coconuts, there are others, many others. Some are very similar to this world, so similar it would be hard to tell them apart. Some are sweeter, yet some are rotten."

Changa's eyes narrowed. He wanted to dismiss Sayidana's words but his experiences proved to him that many things existed beyond the senses.

"Just like these coconuts touch, these worlds touch too," Sayidana continued. "These points of contacts are called gates. There are some who have the ability to travel through these gates. He is one of those who can; so am I."

"So, when you told me you were from far away..." Changa began.

"I meant I am from another world," Sayidana finished. "We are travelers."

Sayidana stood then continued walking down the path. Changa followed, pushing away the questions flooding his mind. He knew better than to seek deeper answers. All he needed to know was what to do to keep his men safe and leave Kilwa Milikiya.

"Sayidana is not my true name," the woman continued. "It is what I call myself here. My world is very different from yours."

"So why did you leave?" Changa asked.

"I had no choice," Sayidana answered. "Travelers are driven to travel. We are born with wanderlust. Passing through worlds also exposes us to different abilities. Some of us use them to help others, some to help themselves. And then there are those who stay silent, content to travel and observe."

"Does this adversary of yours have a name as well?" Changa asked.

"He does, but you could not pronounce it," Sayidana said. "Besides, some say to speak His name is to summon his wrath. We travelers have our own superstitions."

They crested a steep hill overlooking a deep valley sliced by a narrow river.

"We will rest here tonight," Sayidana said. "It is a safe place and easy to defend."

"We should probably sleep in shifts," Changa suggested.

"That won't be necessary," Sayidana said. "You and your men killed the nyani and the inpundulu must rest to regain its strength. Tonight will be peaceful. Our days ahead will be much more interesting."

Changa remained awake long after Sayidana slept, worry and guilt refusing him rest. His decision to come the tainted island revealed his inexperience. Maybe if he had studied his situation long he could have found another way to redeem his losses. But he had chosen what he thought would be a quick way to clear his debts. His life and the lives of his crew were in danger now. Belay's sons were right; he was not fit to be a merchant. When...if they returned to Mombasa he would sell the business to the sons then hire himself out. A man should know his place, the saying goes. Changa had discovered his.

He finally slept. A warm breeze rustled the coconut canopies, the occasional call of an animal in the distance breaking the silence. Changa was awakened by a gentle touch to his cheek. He opened his eyes to Sayidana hovering over him. She straddled him, her nude body almost touching him.

"It has been so long since a man has touched me," she said, her voice echoing in his head. "You can have me, if you wish."

She wrapped her arms around his neck, pressing her body against his. Changa reacted instinctively, his arms embracing her waist and pulling her close. She nuzzled against his neck, nipping his skin with her teeth.

"Changa!"

The shrill cry pierced his ears. It was Sayidana's voice screaming from a distance, yet she lay atop him.

"Changa! It's not me! Free yourself!"

The gentle grip around his neck became a painful hold. He felt pain as the thing pretending to be Sayidana bit into his neck with a snarl. Changa gripped the thing's neck then forced its head away. He rolled until he was on top, pushing it further away. It thrashed under him, its face transforming into that of a bird-like visage. With a cry it shoved Changa away. Changa scrambled to his feet, ready to defend himself. The being continued to transform into a giant bird, resembling the money eagles of the interior. It jumped upward then with a snap of its wings ascended into the dark sky. It let out another blood chilling cry as it flew north.

Changa's neck wound burned like fire as he swayed then fell to the ground. The real Sayidana rushed to him.

"What...what was that?" Changa said, his energy waning with each second.

"It was the inpundulu," Sayidana said. She squatted beside Changa, her hands working furiously.

"How?"

"When the inpundulu is weak it must feed," Sayidana said. "If its master cannot feed it, it fends for itself. It prefers human blood."

Changa fell to his back, the burning more intense.

"Can you..."

"Yes," Sayidana replied.

Something cool pressed against his wound and the burning subsided.

"You are lucky. The inpundulu wasn't able to inject a full dose of venom. This poultice will take most of it away. I'm afraid some had entered your system. You'll be weak for some time. We'll stay here until you'll ready to travel."

Changa could only nod. He closed his eyes and let the darkness take him.

When Changa awoke his energy had returned. Sayidana sat beside him preparing a meal of coconuts and bananas. It was noon, the warm sun shining from overhead, its heat coaxing the moisture from the forest which gathered on his skin. He grunted as he sat up; Sayidana turned toward him then smiled.

"Good," she said. "I was beginning to worry."

"How long did I sleep?" Changa asked.

"Two days," she replied. "One more day and I would have had to continue without you."

She handed Changa the fruit and he ate voraciously.

"I thought you said you could not do it alone."

"I can't," Sayidana replied. "I was going back to the city. Your big friend seems a worthy companion."

"Yusef? He's good enough. Not as good as me, but he'll do."

"You are a man with pride," Sayidana commented.

"You must be to be a merchant," he replied.

"And a warrior," Sayidana said.

"Pride can kill the best warrior," Changa replied.

Sayidana smiled. "Then I chose the right person. Come, we must be on our way."

They finished their meals then continued their trek. They worked their way down into the valley then crossed the broad yet shallow river. The climb up the opposite slopes was taxing but they continued without rest. As they emerged from the vale a large compound rose over the trees a short distance away.

"That's the gate," Sayidana said. "We must hurry to reach it before dark."

"Why before dark?" Changa asked.

"If we are not within those walls before dark we are doomed. There is much worse than nyani and inpundulu protecting the gate."

They ran the entire distance, Changa's attention vacillating between the looming compound and the setting sun. As they neared the compound's door the sound of breaking branches reached his ears. A nauseous pang welled in his stomach; he pulled his sword and a throwing knife then turned toward the sound.

Sayidana stopped at the gate. She approached Changa, a puzzled look on her face.

"There is something coming," she said. "It feels different. I do not know this threat."

"I do," Changa replied. "Go inside."

"What is it?" Sayidana asked.

"Something from my past," Changa said.

The tebo burst into the clearing in the form of a massive gorilla, dragging a small tree in its right hand. It slammed the tree against the ground as it grunted and bared its large fangs. Changa swayed from side to side, bracing himself for the charge.

"Changa!" Sayidana called out. "I can help!"

"No, you can't!" Changa shouted back. "Get inside!"

The tebo roared then charged, the tree rose over its head. Changa roared back then sprinted toward the beast, his eyes on the descending tree. He waited until the last moment before leaping to his right, throwing his knife as he dodged the tree club. The tebo howled as the knife struck its neck and the tree slammed into the dirt. Changa rolled on his shoulder to his feet then ran at the beast again, another throwing knife and sword at the ready. The gorilla-beast yanked the knife from its throat, flinging it into the woods. Changa threw another knife; the beast smacked it away. The distraction gave Changa enough time to hack the back of the creature's left leg, severing its hamstring. The creature struck out, its huge hand crashing into Changa. His sword flew from his hand as he rose from the ground, landing in the forest's edge. Changa blinked in pain, trying to regain his eyesight when the tebo grabbed his arm then lifted him high. Changa reacted, snatching a dagger from his belt then plunging it into the beast's hand. Changa fell; the tebo shook its injured hand as it staggered backwards. Changa clambered to his feet, limping to his sword. He followed the tebo, determined to end the fight. He took a deep breath then ran at the tebo again. With a yell he jumped, smashing into the tebo's chest. Gripping the beast's hair with his free hand, he pulled himself upward until he looked into the tebo's malevolent eyes. The tebo's arms wrapped around Changa, but before the beast could crush him Changa plunged his sword into the beast's throat. A garbled cry seeped from the tebo's mouth, its fetid breath washing over Changa's face. Changa pushed his sword deeper until it protruded from the back of the tebo's neck. He twisted the handle then yanked it free. The tebo's head jerked back, its arms falling limp as it fell backwards onto its back taking Changa down with it.

Changa lay on the dead creature's torso for a moment as the pain in his ribs subsided. He sheathed his sword then rolled off the tebo, barely landing on his feet. When he looked up Sayidana gazed at him, a slight smile on her face.

"You are hard to kill," she said.

A sharp cry from above caught their attention. They looked up to see the inpundulu circling, dark clouds spreading from its wings.

"Inside! Hurry!" Sayidana said.

Changa and Sayidana ran to the entrance. Changa grasped the handle then jerked the door open, surprised it was unbolted. They entered as a barrage of lighting descended from the black clouds, pummeling the stone structure. The walls shuddered as Changa and Sayidana ran down the wide corridor in darkness. Another deluge of lightening hammered the building. The walls transformed, the grey stone emitting a faint blue light illuminating the corridor.

"What's happening?" Changa shouted.

"The inpundulu is opening the gate. We must hurry!"

The long corridor led to a wide cylindrical room. In the center of the room the granite floor shimmered like the surface of a lake, its color the same as the walls. The surface began splashing violently. A human like head emerged; pitch black with eyes that burned like the sun. It rose from the liquid like surface, the figure of a man made of blackness and stars.

"Sayidana," it said. "I should have killed you."

Changa stood motionless as Sayidana walked onto the wavering surface. Her clothes and head wrap merged into her skin as she became like the man standing before.

"Yes, you should have," she replied.

They attacked each other, the force of their clashed creating a shock wave that flattened Changa onto his back. He scrambled back onto his feet then watched as the travelers battled each other with an alacrity that made them seem as blurs. Then they stopped, the male being grasping Sayidana by the throat as he lifted her off her feet.

"I will finish you this time," he said.

Changa threw his knife. He acted on instinct; sure his mortal blade would make no difference in this celestial battle. But he was wrong. The blade bit into his shoulder and he dropped Sayidana, turning his attention to Changa. He yanked the blade from his shoulder.

"What are you...?"

Sayidana appeared behind the man. She grasped his head then twisted it hard. The crack echoed in the chamber; the man slumped then fell into the waves. His form dispersed, tainting the water, then retracted, pooling around Sayidana's feet before being absorbed by her. Changa's throwing knife floated by her feet.

Sayidana picked up the knife then strolled to Changa as she transformed into the woman that he knew. Changa stepped away, his hand going to his sword hilt. It was a foolish move; he doubted if he could protect himself from what he just witnessed.

Sayidana extended the knife to him. Everything about her was the same except her eyes. The cloudy film that once blocked them was gone. Her sepia eyes regarded him.

"You were right," she said. "You were enough."

The building shook, then the ceiling behind them collapsed. The inpundulu struck the simmering stone the slowly sank into the shrinking pool.

"You must leave," Sayidana said. "The gate is closing."

Changa took his knife from Sayidana.

"I believe there was much you did not tell me," he said. "I'm beginning to believe you are the one to be feared."

Sayidana smiled. "It doesn't matter now. He is dead and I will go home."

She grasped Changa's face between her hands then kissed him softly. Changa felt a surge of desire that dissipated as quickly as it appeared. He could tell without looking that his wounds were healed.

"There is a compound three streets west of the mosque," Sayidana said. "If you pull up the floors in the veranda you will find what you seek."

The building shook again.

"Time for you to leave, Changa. I hope you live a long life. Maybe I'll see you again in my travels."

"I am no traveler," Changa said.

Sayidana smirked. "You could be."

She turned then followed the pool as it shrank to a small circle. Sayidana faded as the circle disappeared. The compound walls became translucent, the surrounding hills and forest becoming visible to Changa. And then it was all gone. Changa stood in the middle of an open field. There was no sign that the building ever existed.

"I could be?" he whispered. Changa knelt where the building had once stood. He touched his hand to the ground and the grasses shimmered like the floor of the compound. He jerked his hand away as he shook his head.

"No," he said. "I am Changa Diop, merchant of Mombasa."

He stared at the space a moment longer, then turned and walked away.

* * *

Changa entered the outskirts of Kilwa Milikiya under a noonday sun. The abandoned city was quiet, but Changa knew his men still lived. He'd seen signs along the way of felled trees and animal remains which meant they were following his orders. His feelings were confirmed as he neared the mosque; Yusef and the others emerged single file.

"I thought I told you to build a dhow, Yusef!" Changa shouted.

The big man jerked around so fast he almost fell.

"Kibwana! You're alive!"

The baharia cheered as they ran to him. They lifted him off his feet, parading around the mosque three times before finally placing him down and smothering him with hugs. Yusef was the last to greet him.

"We thought you were dead!" he said. "We were sure Sayidana killed you."

"As you can see that's not the case."

Yusef frowned. "Where is she?"

"She's gone home as we should," Changa said. "How are the dhow repairs coming?"

"There was no need for that," a familiar voice said.

Niko walked up to Changa.

"My conscience would not let me rest," he said. "I had to be with my brothers. I gathered a skeleton crew then set out a week after you. I see that it was more than guilt."

Changa hugged Niko. "It's good to see you." "Now we can leave this damned city!" Yusef said.

"Not yet," Changa said. "You forgot why we came."

Yusef raised his hands. "There is nothing here, bwana. They took everything with them!"

"Not quite," Changa said. He looked about to get his bearing then set off at a trot. When he arrived at the third compound he entered the overgrown courtyard then walked up to the veranda.

"Does anyone have a shovel?" Changa asked.

Moments later a baharia arrived with a makeshift shovel. Changa dug through the sand and shell mix until he struck something hard. The others immediately set about digging, revealing a large mahogany box. It took the entire crew another hour to dig out the container. Changa broke the rusted lock with his sword hilt then opened the box. The container was filled with ivory and bags of gold dust.

"We are saved!" Yusef shouted.

The baharia broke out into a celebration dance. Changa sat and exhaled. He'd found what he came for. His business was spared. He looked up into the cloud stained sky then closed his eyes.

"Thank you, Belay for your teaching and wisdom. Thank you Sayidana for your gift."

He opened his eyes, jumped to his feet, then danced with his men.

THE DEVIL'S LAIR

Zakee and Mustafa circled each other, their focus unwavering. Sweat covered their bodies, running from their bare chests to soak the rim of their cotton pants. Both had removed their turbans long ago, Zakee's youthful black mane in contrast to Mustafa's grey speckled crown. The Old Moor, as he was known in Yemen, was a man whose vitality belied his age and whose skill with the scimitar was legendary. Zakee's father paid the man handsomely to leave his comfortable home in Granada and train his sons. Sultan Basheer ibn Raheem had grand plans for them and was determined they would receive the best in everything.

Mustafa lunged at Zakee, his scimitar flashing toward the young amir's leg. Amir slid his lead foot back then immediately countered with a lunge of his own. Mustafa knocked his blade aside then slashed at Zakee's throat. Zakee pivoted on his rear foot, taking him out of range of Mustafa's attack. Before he could bring his right leg down Mustafa swept his left leg. Zakee crashed onto his back then tried to roll away. Mustafa's blade was at his throat before he could move.

"Never weaken your foundation!" Mustafa said.

"But I have seen you do it, mudarris," Zakee said.

"You are not me," Mustafa replied.

Mustafa sheathed his sword then gave Zakee a hand.

"Again," he said.

Zakee's shoulders slumped. "Mudarris, we have trained most of the day. I have other studies and I am tired."

"Do you think your enemy will care if you are tired?" Mustafa said. "Do you think he will let your rest and sip water from his well?"

Zakee sighed. "We will continue then."

"No," Mustafa said. "You do have duties. Go. We will continue tomorrow."

Zakee bowed to hide his grin.

"Thank you," he said.

Mustafa grunted then waved him away.

Zakee was still full of energy as he hurried from the training room to the baths. He bathed quickly then hurried to the meeting room. There his father sat on his cushions flanked by his viser and his personal bodyguard. His brothers sat before him; they turned their heads and shared their disappointment with his lateness through the frowns on their faces. His father's reaction was different. His smile was generous and welcoming.

"Zakee is here. Good!" he said. "Now we can begin."

A servant placed Zakee's cushion beside his brothers and he sat.

"I am sorry, father," he said. "This morning's practice was intense."

His father nodded. "Mustafa is a master swordsman."

"And expensive," his viser added.

"A small price to pay to make sure Zakee is well trained."

"Why did you not hire him to train us, father?"

Wazeer, his oldest brother, asked the question. His father frowned at him.

"Had I known of Mustafa during your training I would have hired him," his father said. "I did not. Do you have any more questions before I continue, Wazeer?"

Wazeer lowered his head. "No father, I don't."

His father looked to Khalid, his second oldest brother, Khalid. His nervous natured brother wrung his hands.

"I... I have no questions, father," he said.

"Good. Your grandfather has summoned us north. A minor chieftain has obtained a blasphemous object that has given him the power to rally the Scattered Clans. He has claimed the title of Sultan and vowed to march on Sana'a. We are to bring warriors to support him."

"What is this object that gives such power," Zakee asked.

"It is a jade obelisk," his father said. "It is said it possesses the power of the old gods."

Khalid's eyes widened. "There is no god before Allah!"

"That is true," his father said. "Which is why we march north tomorrow."

Wazeer cleared his throat. "How is it that grandfather can command you to march with him against this charlatan? He is not the sultan. This sounds like a local disturbance. It should be handled as such."

His father answered Wazeer with a glare.

"Take care of your business. As I said, we depart tomorrow."

The sons bowed then stood to leave the room.

"Zakee, stay a moment," his father said.

The glances Zakee received from his brothers were not pleasant. He wanted to be closer to them but the potential of becoming sultan after their father's death created a distance between them that widened by his father's preference for him. It was not attention he asked for nor was he comfortable with it. His brothers were older and more capable in his opinion. His father's attention was due to his mother being his favored wife.

Zakee approached his father then bowed.

"What is it, father?"

"This will be your first time in battle," he said. "Your mother would be vexed with me if you died."

Zakee's chest tightened as he looked up at his father.

"I am ready," he said.

"You're as ready as you can be," his father said. "Mustafa said you are a fast learner and a skilled swordsman. That does not guarantee your safety in war."

"What do you wish to tell me, father?"

"Tomorrow I will assign Wazeer and Khalid command of two units of the army. You will march with me."

Zakee's shook his head with disappointment.

"How will I learn to command men by your side?"

"By watching," his father replied. "I have another assignment for you as well."

Zakee's mood perked. "What is it, father?"

"Your grandfather was once a great warrior, but no man wins against time. He is older and feebler than he will admit. He will ride with us as well, but he needs a strong sword beside him in case the war reaches him."

"He has his bodyguards," Zakee said.

"They are as old as him," his father said. "I wish for you to stay with him during the heat of battle. It will bring me much pleasure if you agree to do so."

"I will do as you ask, father. But I am not happy about it."

He looked into his father's smiling face.

"It is all I can ask," his father said.

* * *

The army set out from Sana'a at sunrise immediately after morning prayers. Zakee rode with his father and brothers, barely able to contain his excitement. This was his first excursion beyond the city, every mile a revelation. They traveled for three days north, deeper into the desert. On the fifth day they arrived at his grandfather's city, a modest collection of stone buildings nestled in the center of an oasis. His grandfather's palace towered over the surrounding homes, its only rival the nearby mosque with its single minaret. Servants met them as they neared, supplying them with fresh food and water while they relieved them of their gear. One servant approached them, a tall man with piercing eyes and dark skin.

"Welcome," the man said, his voice rich and melodious. I am Jamal ibn Sayeed. My master awaits your presence."

"Lead the way," Zakee's father said.

The quartet followed Jamal into his grandfather's palace. Although the building was small compared to his father's abode, the innards bulged with a wide variety of riches; Persian rugs, carved ivory artifacts and displays of jewels from nearby and across the seas. Zakee moved closer to his father then tugged at his shirt.

"Grandfather is very rich," he whispered.

His father grunted. "My father's weakness is his desire for wealth. When he was a young man he traveled the ends of the earth gathering such things. As he aged he sent me and my brothers on such quests. Once we were men with our own families he sent his servants."

"I think I will go on my own quests as well," Zakee said.

"One challenge as a time, young lion," he father said. "Besides, such behavior is unbecoming for a good Muslim. But we all have our sins to bear."

Jamal led them into his grandfather's sitting chamber. The old patriarch sat on a pile of silk cushions combing his beard as a musician played a relaxing tune on a stringed instrument Zakee did not recognize.

"Master," Jamal announced. "Your family has arrived."

His grandfather head jerked up and a wide grin came to his face. He looked far younger than his age, a trait strong among their family. He jumped up from his pillows then strode to them with his arms wide.

"Basheer!" his grandfather exclaimed.

The men hugged then kissed each other's cheeks.

"It is so good that you came," grandfather said. "Your brothers are cowards."

His father grinned. "They are not cowards, father. They are busy."

"Too busy to help their father defend the Faith? No one is that busy."

"I am here, father," Basheer said. "It will have to do."

His grandfather shrugged his shoulders.

"I see you have brought the cubs," he said.

He embraced each of Zakee's brothers. He stopped before Zakee, a shocked look on his face.

"Is this Zakee who stands before me?"

Zakee embraced then kissed his grandfather.

"It is I, grandfather," he said.

His grandfather held him at arm's length.

"The last time I saw you your mother held you wrapped in blankets. Now you stand before me as a man. Basheer, what kind of man is your youngest son?"

"He is man of faith and intelligence," his father answered. "I am proud to call him my son."

Zakee glanced at his father and smiled.

"And is he an effective defender of the Faith?"

"That remains to be seen," his father answered truthfully.

"Ah!" his grandfather said. "You will ride beside me, Zakee. Together we will march into the Devil's lair and end his blasphemy!"

"As you wish, grandfather," Zakee replied.

"Excellent!" his grandfather said. "I offer you all my hospitality. Rest and relax while I gather my forces. We will march in seven days!"

While his father and brothers took grandfather's words to heart, Zakee spent every moment ranging the borders of the oasis kingdom. Every inch was effectively managed, producing an abundance of goods for the inhabitants. He spent time with his grandmother, listening to stories about his uncles, aunts and most of all, his father. It seems he was mischievous boy and the bane of his siblings. It was a happy day for them when he finally departed to seek his own fortune since he was not the oldest.

As the sun rose on the day of departure Zakee awoke filled with anxious energy. He dressed quickly, gathered his weapons and armor then emerged from his room into the narrow hallway.

"Well, well, well!" his grandfather said. "I see one cub is eager for the hunt."

Zakee turned to see his grandfather dressed and armored, flanked by two elderly bodyguards.

"I am, grandfather," he said.

One of the bodyguards frowned.

"Do not be so joyful," he said. "War is an ugly thing."
His grandfather waved his hand.

"Don't listen to Abdul," he said. "He is an old man who would rather sit in his room and study the stars than fight for the glory of his sultan."

"I am wise enough to know my best days are done," he said.

"Be quiet, Abdul," grandfather said. "Zakee need not hear you whining."

"I am glad to be off to battle," the other bodyguard said.

"See?" His grandfather put his arm around the bodyguard's shoulders.

"Selim is a warrior!"

Selim nodded his gray head. "I'd rather die with a sword in my hand than a weak old man in my bed."

"Enough talk," grandfather said. "We'll rouse the others and be on our way."

The expeditionary forces gathered outside the palace gates after morning prayers. Zakee met with his brother and fathers, their mood much more subdued. His father placed his hands heavy on Zakee's shoulders.

"This is no game, son," he said. "You are skilled but you have never fought to the death. There must be no hesitation in your actions. Do you understand?"

"I do, father," Zakee replied.

"Stay close to your grandfather," he said. "Let no harm come to him."

"I will, father," Zakee said.

The expedition waited until dusk before beginning their journey. Zakee rode beside his grandfather surrounded by aging and inexperienced warriors. Their appearance shook his confidence. He looked to his father and brothers then felt somewhat better. The best of Sana'a had come to his father's call. It was his father's plan that they would act as vanguard and bear the brunt of the fighting. His grandfather's warriors were along mostly for ceremony. Zakee's feelings were mixed; he was honored to be asked to protect his grandfather but disappointed that he was not part of the vanguard. It was possible he would see no fighting at all.

They marched north for five days. On the night of the fifth day scouts were deployed for details of their objective. The news they delivered was sobering.

"Their army is much larger than ours," Akil said. "They surround their temple continuously."

"Are they all warriors?" his father asked.

Akil took a sip of water from his bag. "No. Most seemed to be farmers. Their weapons are their farm tools. The true warriors are positioned closest to the temple."

His father nodded as he pulled at his beard.

"We must strike quick and hard," he said. "The cavalry will charge through them to the temple. The footmen will follow, disrupting pursuit. Once the farmers are scattered they will join us attacking the temple."

"Our objective is the obelisk," grandfather said. "We will have wasted our time if we don't obtain it."

Everyone nodded in agreement.

"May Allah be with us," his father said.

The warriors moved into position during the night. The black horizon was pierced by a pulsing green light emanating from the temple.

"It is the obelisk," Akil said. "It beats like the heart. Some say it is alive."

"Nonsense," Zakee's grandfather said. "Tricks that fool the mind and eye. Tomorrow we will put an end to them."

Zakee looked away from his grandfather then to the light. It seemed to grow closer the longer he gazed at it. A hand touched his shoulder, breaking his concentration.

"Do not look at it too long, master," Akil said. "It will steal your soul!"

Zakee scrambled to his feet then dusted off his clothes.

"Impossible," he said. "Like my grandfather said, tricks to fool the mind and eye."

He stomped away, doubting his own words.

The next day began with a silent muster. The men had been briefed the day before so there was no need for words. The cavalry took the vanguard, followed by the foot soldiers carrying shields and spears. Zakee rode in the rear with his grandfather and his warriors, his grandfather's displeasure visibly apparent as he jerked about in his saddle.

"This is an insult!" he finally said. "I should be leading this attack!"

Zakee searched for the right words to sooth him and was relieved when Abdul spoke.

"We are old men," he said. "Allow us a few more moments of life."

His grandfather spat. "You disgust me, Abdul!"

Abdul grinned. "Not for much longer."

His words made his grandfather smile. He turned to Zakee.

"Remember this day, Zakee," he said. "It will be glorious."

A ragged chorus of horns echoed from the distance.

"They've seen us," Selim said. "The game begins."

The cavalry charged. The foot soldiers trotted behind them, shields raised and spears lowered. Zakee stood up in his saddle to peer over those before him. A line men and women ran toward the cavalry, waving their weapons of their heads.

"Protect the light!" they shouted.

The cavalry crashed into the worshippers. A few riders tumbled from their mounts and were hacked to death by the throng. The mass of riders cut through the disorganized defenders, riding unhindered to the temple. The foot soldiers arrived to support the cavalry just as the defenders turned to pursue. Zakee saw his father and brothers riding toward the temple and wished he was with them.

"Come!" his grandfather shouted. "Glory awaits us!"

"Grandfather, no!" Zakee shouted.

Grandfather galloped away, pursued by his retinue. Zakee recovered from his shock then followed. The foot soldiers made way as they rode through then plunged into the ragged protectors of the temple. Zakee drew his scimitar, his hand tight on his. His horse sped through the hostile throng too fast for any to attack him, although a few attempted to throw spears or shoot arrows at him. Soon they could see his father and the cavalry, their progress stalled by the temple's trained warriors. Zakee hoped his grandfather would stop, but his hopes were unheeded. He worked his way through the melee, striking down two defenders then urging his mount up the steep steps to the entrance of the temple. Zakee was so focused on his grandfather he almost lost his life.

"Zakee!" his father shouted.

Zakee looked in the direction of his father's voice to see a temple defender galloping toward him, his scimitar raised.

"Defend the temple!" he shouted. "Defend the Obelisk!"

Zakee managed to raise his scimitar as their horses crashed together. He blocked the powerful down stroke, the shock coursing down his arm into his shoulder. Zakee knocked the second blow aside then slashed at the man's face. The defender jerked his head back, the tip of Zakee's blade nipping the man's chin and drawing blood. Zakee hesitated; never had he cut a person with his blade. The defender stabbed at Zakee's throat; Zakee leaned to his left then slashed the man under his arm. The defender pulled his horse away, clinching arm against his body then falling from his horse.

"Zakee! Get to your grandfather now!" his father shouted again.

Zakee spurred his horse toward the temple, his body shaking. The horse carried him up the stairs with ease, reaching the entrance as Selim and Abdul struck down the guards defending the doors. They dismounted then pulled the doors open. As soon as they remounted the trio rode into the temple.

Zakee followed. He was swallowed by intense green light then struck hard by an invisible force. He fell from his horse then lost his breath as he struck the marble floor. It took a moment for him to regain his breath; when he did he fought to regain his feet, scimitar in hand.

Grandfather, Selim and Abdul lay on the floor. Selim laid still, a pool of blood spreading from under his head. Abdul moaned as he clutched his right arm. Grandfather cursed as he struggled to stand. A figure loomed over him, a man covered in a hooded robe, his pale face grooved with scarification. The man gripped the jade obelisk like a sword as he raised it over his head, a grim smile on his face.

"You want the obelisk, Sala? Then you shall have it!"

Zakee lunged at the priest. He winced as the obelisk grazed his back just before he crashed into the startled man. They rolled across the marble floor, finally ending a tangled heap. Zakee was the first to free himself and regain his feet; the priest turned onto his back, the jade obelisk still in his hand.

He stabbed the object at Zakee. It flared and a ray of green energy streaked at the young warrior. Zakee dodged to his right then struck at the priest's face. The priest swung the obelisk, blocking his blade. The nefarious light brushed his shoulder, burning his shirt. Zakee yelped then jumped away, using his free hand to rip off his shirt.

The priest was on his feet. He slashed at Zakee again; Zakee threw his shirt at the priest for a desperate diversion. His shirt met the green light then burst into flames. The sudden explosion was the distraction he needed. He spun to his left then sliced down. His blade struck the priest's obelisk bearing arm, cutting off his hand just above the wrist.

"Aiee!!!"

Zakee expected the priest to fall to the floor clutching his arm. Instead the crazed man lunged at him, waving his bloody stump.

"You will never have the obelisk!" he screamed.

Zakee gripped his scimitar with both hand then chopped at the priest's neck. The priest's head fell backwards, a grimace frozen on his face. The headless body fell forward into Zakee, blood splashing his jerkin and pants. He stumbled away as he shoved the body aside. He took another step back then tripped over his grandfather, landing on his backside.

"Zakee! Father!"

Zakee turned to see his father and brothers running to them, followed by the other warriors. Zakee stood then swayed, his energy depleted. He looked down at his torso then realized that the blood was his, not the priest.

"Father," he managed to say before passing out into his father's outstretched arms.

Zakee awoke in his bed. He attempted to sit up then winced. He was bare chested and tucked snug under silk sheets. He lifted the sheets to see a wide bandage across his midsection. The details of the temple attack slowly came back to him, but he still could not remember how he was wounded.

"It was a dagger."

Mustafa swaggered into the room, a slight grin on his face.

"Always watch both of your opponent's hands, even if you've cut the other one off," he said.

Zakee smiled as he sat up in the bed.

"I'm sorry, master," he said. "I should have been more attentive."

Mustafa sat on Zakee's bed then pulled back the sheets, examining his bandage.

"This is lesson enough," he said. "There is no better teacher than experience. So, you are a great man now. You beheaded the evil priest and saved your grandfather's life."

Zakee's cheeks warmed and the looked away.

"It was Allah's will," he said.

"But your skills," Mustafa answered.

Mustafa stood then folded his arms across his chest.

"My time with you is complete. There is no more I can teach you. Once a man goes to battle and lives he is trained enough. But don't forget to practice."

"Where are you going?" Zakee asked.

"Back to Al Andulus, or at least to what is left of it. Your father has grand plans for you. Don't let him down. Goodbye, Zakee. May Allah protect you."

Mustafa strode for the door.

"Wait!" Zakee called out. "What plans?"

* * *

Zakee sat at his desk, reading over the daily report as his ministers waited patiently for his approval. He glanced up, looking beyond them to the view of the harbor through his window. It had been two years since his father made him governor of Aden, his reward for Zakee's valor. His brothers were not happy about his selection for they were older and by right should have been given a governorship before him. But his father made his decision and no one would defy him.

Zakee turned his attention back to the parchments before him. He was about to stamp them with his seal when he was interrupted.

Sahib! Sahib! There is a ship in the harbor!

Zakee looked up at the servant. The man's face dripped sweat, his chest heaving for breath.

"There are always ships in the harbor," he said.

"Not like this one!"

The servant ran to the window, the others following. Zakee leaned back on his stool. The others let out a collective gasp.

"Zakee, you should see this!"

Zakee went to the window and was startled by what he saw. A black ship rested just beyond the docks. Its white sails bulged with the western monsoon winds. He turned about then strode from the room, his mind racing with questions. The others followed, their chatter about the mysterious ship stirring more questions.

His horse and personal guard were waiting as he entered the courtyard. Jamal, the commander of his forces approached him as he mounted his horse.

"Zakee, this isn't safe," he said. "This may be an attacking force."

"Then why did you have my horse ready," he asked.

"Because I knew you would want to go see for yourself," Jamal answered.

Zakee looked at Jamal then smiled. "Then let's go see."

They galloped through the city, gathering onlookers and they neared the docks. By the time they reached the docks half the city trailed them. Zakee dismounted and his guards pushed away the beggars and others wishing to approach him. The guards along the docks had anticipated his arrival and cleared the docks of everyone except those essential. A slim boat rowed by eight bare armed men eased to the dock. As the boat reached the mooring figure stood, its body covered completely in an emerald robed, the jeweled hood covering its features. The helmsman on the boat jumped the distance between the boat and the docks, securing the vessel with a thick braided leather rope. The figure waited as the others climbed onto the deck. They wore swords at their waists with circular pommels.

"Zakee, please stand behind us," Jamal asked.

Zakee moved behind his guards. The others came forward, the robed figure sauntering behind them. The guards met, Jamal glaring at his counterpart.

"You have entered the city of Aden," Jamal said. "Who are you and what is your purpose here?"

The mysterious guards parted. The figure came forward then removed its hood.

Zakee gasped, as did the others. She was the most beautiful woman he'd ever seen. Her hair formed a black halo about her head, her ebony skin flawless. She looked past Jamal with intense hazel eyes, setting her gaze on him and summoning him forward. Zakee pushed his guards aside. He almost knelt when he finally stood before her, his breath short like one stricken by love.

"Who are you?" he managed to ask.

"I am Bahati, queen of the Zanj," she said. Her voice chimed like a thousand beautiful bells.

Zakee swallowed. "Why are you here?"

Bahati smiled. "I seek an artifact of grave importance for my people."

Zakee looked puzzled. "What is it that you seek?"

Bahati's smile faded. "An obelisk," she said. "A jade obelisk."

Before The Safari

ABOUT THE AUTHOR

Milton Davis is a Black Speculative fiction writer and owner of MVmedia, LLC, a small publishing company specializing in Science Fiction, Fantasy and Sword and Soul. MVmedia's mission is to provide speculative fiction books that represent people of color in a positive manner. Milton is the author of seventeen novels; his most recent is the Sword and Soul adventure *Son of Mfumu*. He is the editor and co-editor of seven anthologies; *The City, Dark Universe* with Gene Peterson; *Griots: A Sword and Soul Anthology and Griot: Sisters of the Spear*, with Charles R. Saunders; *The Ki Khanga Anthology,* the *Steamfunk! Anthology*, and the *Dieselfunk anthology* with Balogun Ojetade. MVmedia has also published *Once Upon A Time in Afrika* by Balogun Ojetade and *Abegoni: First Calling* and *Nyumbani Tales* by Sword and Soul creator and icon Charles R. Saunders. Milton's work had also been featured in *Black Power: The Superhero Anthology*; Skelos *2: The Journal of Weird Fiction and Dark Fantasy Volume 2, Steampunk Writes Around the World* published by Luna Press and *Bass Reeves Frontier Marshal Volume Two*.

Milton resides in Metro Atlanta with his wife Vickie and his children Brandon and Alana.